A FRAME OF DREAMS

The Marquis of Ruckford was enchanted.

Vanessa was as delicately beautiful as the miniatures she worked so patiently to restore. She was like no other woman the Marquis had ever known. In fact, the more he saw Vanessa, the more he realized life without her would be unthinkable.

Matrimony was not the solution. The Marquis had planned his future carefully. It certainly did not include marriage to an unknown artist's daughter—no matter how lovely.

There was only one arrangement the Marquis could offer Vanessa. As she listened to him phrase it, Vanessa was torn between longing for the man she had grown to love and horror at what he was proposing.

BARBARA CARTLAND

Bantam Books by Barbara Cartland
Ask your bookseller for the books you have missed

A Frame
of
Dreams

Barbara Cartland

BANTAM BOOKS · TORONTO · NEW YORK · LONDON

A FRAME OF DREAMS
A Bantam Book / March 1976

Published simultaneously in the United States and Canada

Bantam Books are published by Bantam Books, Inc. Its trade-
mark, consisting of the words "Bantam Books" and the por-
trayal of a bantam, is registered in the United States Patent
Office and in other countries. Marca Registrada. Bantam
Books, Inc., 666 Fifth Avenue, New York, New York 10019.

PRINTED IN THE UNITED STATES OF AMERICA

Author's Note

The details of the Miniaturists are correct, and Peter Paul Lens, 1714–1750, son of Bernard Lens, 1682–1740, was, as I have described, obliged to leave Ireland hurriedly in 1738, having been censured for his activities in a Hellfire Club by the Irish House of Lords.

Little is known of his subsequent life in England, and he died when he was thirty-six.

I have therefore given him a son—Cornelius Lens —in this story.

Peter Paul Lens has a profile of his father and a very appealing miniature of a "Ragged Little Boy" in the Victoria and Albert Museum, London.

The descriptions of Carlton House and Vauxhall Gardens are completely accurate, and Monsieur André Jacques Garnerin was the inventor of the first practical parachute.

Chapter One

1804

The Marquis of Ruckford permitted his valet to assist him out of his evening-coat. It was exquisitely cut by Weston and fitted without a wrinkle.

At the same time, because the Marquis disliked feeling confined, it was slightly looser than those the same tailor cut for the Prince of Wales.

The bed-chamber, being the best in the Posting-Inn, was large and, despite its low ceilings, exceedingly comfortable.

Although it was now early May, there was a fire burning brightly in the grate and His Lordship noted with satisfaction that the oak four-poster bed was wide and its deep mattress should ensure his comfort.

There was, however, a slight frown on the Marquis's handsome face as in the distance there could be heard the noise of voices and laughter, a sound which had continued all through the evening and had been louder still in the private Parlour where he had eaten his dinner.

"I have never known the place so noisy," the

1

Marquis remarked to his valet. "Perhaps we would
have been better advised to stay with Lord Lincoln!"

"It is unfortunate, M'Lord," the valet replied,
"that there should have been a Mill taking place in
the vicinity on the very day of our arrival. 'Tis said
the purse exceeded two thousand guineas and a large
amount of money was laid on the local man."

"Did he win?" the Marquis asked somewhat in-
differently.

An amateur boxer himself of some distinction, he
found it a bore to watch a Mill unless the very finest
champions had been matched.

There were, in his opinion, far too many over-
boosted fights in country areas which were usually
organised by local Inn-keepers to bring money into
the vicinity.

"I believe, M'Lord," his valet replied, "that the
fight was in fact disappointing. Despite the much-
vaunted qualities of the local man's opponent, he was
floored in under half an hour and with such ease that
the majority of the spectators are complaining they
have come a long way for nothing."

"That is what I expected," the Marquis remarked
laconically. "At the same time, there are too many
guests in the Inn and they are far too loud-mouthed
for my comfort."

"They're drinking themselves under the table,
M'Lord," the valet replied. "The Landlord's never had
such a harvest!"

The Marquis did not reply. He did not like gos-
siping with his servants, and anyway he was tired,
having travelled since early in the morning from Lord
Hargrave's Castle in Huntingdonshire.

As his valet assisted him to remove the rest of
his garments and he washed in the warm water to
which a few drops of eau-de-cologne had been added,
he thought that the Prince of Wales should be grateful that he had undertaken this journey on his behalf.

It had in fact given the Marquis an opportunity
for trying out his new team of perfectly matched
chestnuts, which he had purchased two months be-

fore at Tattersalls and which he had not previously taken farther than Hyde Park. But the whole trip had taken a lot of planning.

Lord Hargrave's Castle was off the main roads, and twisting, dusty lanes did not make for pleasant driving. What was more, it meant that His Lordship had to spend two nights on the journey, one between London and the Castle, and one on his return.

The two nights he had spent in the Castle had been somewhat rewarding in that he had acquired an interesting find to show the Prince of Wales. He had also brought a picture back with him which he knew would delight His Royal Highness.

At the same time, he had not been in the Castle for more than half an hour before he understood Lord Hargrave's disinclination to come to London.

Also that his suggestion that the Marquis of Ruckford should be sent to inspect his treasures had been inspired by a very different motive from what had appeared in his well-expressed letter to the Prince.

Lord Hargrave had produced his daughter with the air of a magician bringing an unexpected rabbit out of a hat.

The Marquis, who was used to such wiles, was irritated to find himself once more in the uncomfortable position of making it absolutely clear that his interest was in paintings and not in marriage.

The Honourable Emily, aged nineteen, had a pleasing countenance. In fact, the Marquis was sure that Lord Hargrave would find it quite easy to procure for her a husband of sufficient wealth and importance to match her dark-eyed attractions.

At the same time, he made it very clear that he was not available in the marriage-market.

It was not surprising, as he would have been frank enough to admit to himself, that Lord Hargrave in aspiring for the best for his daughter should consider him as a suitable son-in-law.

The Marquis had been pursued by every matchmaking father and mother in the length and breadth of Great Britain since the time he had left Eton.

He was not only immensely wealthy and his house, like his Estates, the finest in the land. He was also an extremely attractive man.

Handsome so that only with the greatest dexterity and a certain amount of disagreeableness had he prevented himself from being nicknamed "Beau Ruckford," the Marquis was an outstanding sportsman.

He was almost unique, being admired and liked by his own sex as much as by the lovely ladies who sought his favours.

A noted Corinthian and undoubtedly the finest whip in the "Four-in-Hand" Club, he had made his mark as a duellist not only with swords but also with pistols, and was undoubtedly one of the greatest amateur riders that ever carried his own horses past the winning-post.

Besides all this, he played his part in the House of Lords, and Statesmen valued his opinion and support.

The Prince of Wales not only called the Marquis his friend with an undeniable sincerity, but he also found him an invaluable source of information and discrimination where works of Art were concerned.

The Prince's predilection for paintings, furniture, and everything else which added to the glory of Carlton House supplied the cartoonists with an endless stream of ammunition against him.

He had incurred debts which had infuriated the people and Parliament, but the treasures on which he spent such vast sums were in fact the envy of every connoisseur.

There was no doubt that Carlton House was magnificent!

It had been granted to the Prince by the King as his London residence, provided that he did not give away any of the land and took upon himself "all the repairs, taxes, and the keeping up of the gardens."

The house, which had been built at the beginning of the Eighteenth Century and had formerly been inhabited by the Dowager Princess of Wales, the Prince's grandmother, was unremarkable.

But the Prince employed Holland, the architect of Brook's Club, and by 1783 he had moved into Carlton House to live there as the work went on round him.

It was a delight to the Prince to be able to exercise his excellent taste in decorating the rooms and collecting the furniture.

The objets d'art, pictures, looking-glasses, bronzes, Sèvres china, Gobelin tapestries, and countless other treasures which enriched this "Palace" were to stand comparison with Versailles and even the Palace of St. Petersburg.

He himself scoured the salerooms and Dealers' shops of London, buying week after week objects which he carefully arranged in the various rooms of Carlton House.

Although there was a difference of twelve years in their ages, the Prince counted the Marquis as one of his closest friends, and that he should both encourage and assist him was a continual delight.

The Prince found that the majority of his friends were uninterested in his expensive but rewarding hobby or pretended to appreciate what they did not understand.

The two men were opposites in most other regards.

Both were outstandingly handsome, but while the Prince was growing fatter every year from overindulgence, the Marquis became, if anything, slightly slimmer.

Despite his broad shoulders, his hips were narrow and, as his tailor often told him, there was not a spare ounce of flesh on his whole body.

This accentuated the bone structure of his face and threw into prominence his high cheek-bones and the sharpness of his jaw.

The Prince in his youth had been what was called a "pretty boy," while the Marquis was clear cut, with a jauntiness or perhaps the right word was "raffishness" about him which was very different.

He had, as more than one woman had told him,

the face of a buccaneer, and his behaviour where women were concerned warranted this description.

But while the Prince drifted through life indulging his fancies, being at times outrageously uncontrolled, the Marquis was not only well organised but had a very clear idea of what he desired both now and in the future.

On one point he was completely determined, and that was that he did not intend to marry until it suited him.

He was well aware that, with his historic name, his great possessions, and a social position that was second to none, he must eventually beget an heir to carry on the family.

He had, in fact, although he had not mentioned it to anyone, already selected his bride—the daughter of the Duke of Tealby, whose lands marched with his.

Lady Adelaide Wilmott was exactly the type of wife that the Marquis visualised at the top of his table.

She was quiet, well mannered, and, while not a striking beauty, had undoubtedly a pleasing face.

With her aristocratic features, her straight nose and proudly held head which showed good breeding, the Marquis was aware that she would carry the fabulous Ruckford jewels with an air of distinction.

Lady Adelaide was at present a Lady-in-Waiting to the Queen, and the Marquis felt that such an appointment would give her an insight and training for the life she would live when she became his wife.

The fact that she was already over twenty-four years of age did not perturb him. He found young girls a bore, and he was certain that because Lady Adelaide had remained unmarried for longer than most of her contemporaries, they would have more interests in common.

In the meantime the Marquis enjoyed himself, but unlike the Prince he was quiet and discreet in his love-affairs, and this made him an even more desirable lover in the eyes of the ladies of the social world.

It was one thing for a famous hostess, an acknowledged beauty, the wife of a distinguished nobleman to fall in love; quite another if she should lose her good name irretrievably in doing so.

As Lady Melbourne, the great Whig hostess, had said:

"Anyone who braves the opinion of the world sooner or later feels the consequences of it."

Her own reputation was far from spotless. In fact she had taken a number of lovers, among them Lord Coleraine, the Duke of Bedford, and the most important Lord Egremont. But she never flaunted her conquests in public.

There were a great many suspicions as to where and when the Marquis loved, but it was difficult for those suspicions to be confirmed.

While inevitably he was gossiped about in every Club and in every Drawing-Room of the *Beau-Monde,* what was said was mostly speculation and could very seldom be verified.

Apart from amatory adventures with women of his own class, the Marquis, as was the fashion, had a kept mistress.

It was to be expected that he would choose her with the same care and forethought he expended on anything which concerned his own comfort.

Mariabelle Kerrin had been an outstanding success as Polly Peachum in a revival of the *Beggar's Opera.* The Marquis had watched her and been interested. He had visited her in her dressing-room after the performance and been captivated.

Mariabelle proved herself to be entrancingly experienced in bed and had a roguish wit which amused the Marquis.

She was at first, as he had expected, insatiably avaricious, but lately her demands had not been so insistent and he had the uneasy feeling that she was growing too fond of him.

The moment a woman became possessive or clinging he felt constrained, and found himself impelled to cut any cords which bound him, to be free.

It was an inevitable development in his love-affairs and the Marquis often found himself wonder-

ing if the day would ever come when he would be the
seeker, not the sought—the hunter, not the hunted.

It appeared, on the face of it, to be a very unlikely prospect.

Having finished washing, the Marquis put on his
night-shirt of Chinese silk which had been specially
made for him in Bond Street, and over it a robe of
rich brocade which reached the floor.

He tied round his narrow waist a silk sash with
deep fringes, then dismissed his valet.

"Is there something else you require, M'Lord?"

"Nothing, thank you, Jarvis," the Marquis replied.
"Call me at eight o'clock. I wish to reach London as
early as possible."

"If the traffic isn't too bad, M'Lord, I'm sure Your
Lordship'll set up a new record," the valet said ad-
miringly.

He was a man who had served the Marquis since
he was a boy, and there was no doubt of the adulation
in his eyes as he looked at his Master.

"That would undoubtedly be a satisfaction," the
Marquis admitted. "Lord Derwent has been boasting
for years that he holds the record on this particular
road."

"I'm sure, M'Lord, that he'll not be able to claim
such an achievement in the future," Jarvis replied.

He glanced round the bed-chamber to see that
everything was in place; the bed made up with the
Marquis's own fine linen, lambs'-wool blankets, and
goose-feather pillows.

The mat embroidered with His Lordship's mono-
gram was laid on the floor and a bottle of the water
which came from a mineral spring on his Estate which
had been known to the Romans, stood on a table
with an engraved crystal cut glass beside it.

Carrying the Marquis's discarded clothes over his
arm, the valet opened the door, bowed his head re-
spectfully, and then went out into the passage, closing
the door behind him.

The Marquis picked up *The Morning Post* and
walked towards a winged arm-chair on the hearth-
rug.

He was just about to sit down when he was conscious of a strong draught coming from the window which was undoubtedly chill against his bare ankles.

There had been a cold wind blowing all day, while the sun had appeared fitfully in and out of the clouds, so the Marquis had expected rain.

The high wind had, however, prevented this, but towards evening it had grown unmistakably chill.

Now putting down the newspaper on the chair, the Marquis walked across the room to where rose-patterned chintz curtains concealed a bow-window which overlooked the garden at the back of the Inn.

The Marquis stepped through the curtains to find, as he had expected, that one of the diamond-paned casements was wide open. He closed it, setting the catch in place, and thought that before he went to bed he would open it again.

Outside, the clouds had cleared away and the sky was full of stars. The trees surrounding the Inn were bending in the wind and the Marquis told himself that it would be another blustery day tomorrow, which might reduce his speed towards London.

Down below him, the uncurtained windows threw golden lights into the garden. Shadows moved across them and again he could hear the noise of those revelling below.

He hoped it would not disturb his sleep and, turning from the window, he opened the curtains and returned to the fireside.

As he did so he saw, on the other side of the room, the door onto the passage open and a small figure in white come through it.

It was a woman!

As the Marquis stood staring in surprise she closed the bed-room door behind her and quickly turned the key in the lock.

Then she stood looking at the door and the Marquis had the impression that she was listening.

Resolutely he walked forward.

"I have a feeling, Madam," he said coldly, "that you have come to the wrong room."

The woman started and then with an exclamation

turned round to face him. He saw that she was very young and very pretty.

She had an oval face with large grey-green eyes, and her hair, which fell to well below her shoulders, was pale gold with touches of red in it.

She stared at the Marquis as he advanced towards her; then as if she found her voice with difficulty she said hesitatingly:

"I . . . I am sorry . . . I looked in . . . and thought the . . . room was . . . empty."

The Marquis was just about to reply when suddenly there was the sound of footsteps outside the door, followed by a loud knock.

The girl started again and the Marquis saw an expression of terror in her face as two hands went out towards him and she touched his arm.

"Please . . . please," she whispered, so low that he only just heard the words. "Hide me! I will explain, but please . . . hide me!"

The Marquis hesitated.

He had no desire to be caught up in some romantic drama and he realised that the girl beside him was wearing only her night-gown with a white shawl covering it.

He was about to say that much to his regret he could have no part in what must be a private matter between her and whoever was outside the door, but the terror in her face combined with her pleading for help made him hesitate.

There was no doubt that the girl was very young, and as the knock came again, loud, peremptory, and to the Marquis, impertinent, he made up his mind.

He pointed to the curtains from which he had just emerged and moving swiftly and silently she ran across the room to disappear from view.

Slowly and without haste the Marquis unlocked the door.

Outside stood a man he recognised as Sir Julius Stone, whom he had always disliked.

The two men stared at each other for a moment.

"Ruckford!" Sir Julius ejaculated. "I was not expecting to find you here!"

"I am on the point of retiring," the Marquis replied icily.

Sir Julius's eyes went past him into the room.

In his late thirties, Julius Stone was, in the Marquis's estimation, one of the less reputable and certainly more unpleasant Bucks who frequented the gambling Clubs of St. James's.

He came from an aristocratic family and there was nothing wrong with his antecedents, but he had made his name a by-word for licentiousness, brawling, and rowdiness, which had been characteristic of quite a number of the young bloods at the end of the century.

There were a great many unsavoury stories current about Sir Julius, but they did not interest the Marquis and he was not concerned with the Baronet's morals, good or bad.

He only knew that he had nothing in common with such a man, and although they met occasionally at Carlton House and encountered each other at White's or Watiers, they were no more than nodding acquaintances.

There was a pause and then as if Sir Julius was choosing his words he said:

"I saw someone enter this room a few moments ago—a woman!"

The Marquis raised his eye-brows.

"The lighting in the passage is obviously misleading. I imagine that you saw my valet. Good-night, Stone!"

He would have shut the door but Sir Julius put his shoulder against it.

"One minute, Ruckford!" he said. "I am not in the habit of questioning the sight of my own eyes. I saw a woman come in here and she is mine!"

"Are you doubting my word?" the Marquis asked.

Although he did not raise his voice something in the tone of it and the expression in his eyes made Sir Julius step back.

"I was sure—completely sure!" he muttered.

"Good-night, Stone!" the Marquis said again, and closing the door locked it.

He waited where he was and was aware a few seconds later that the curtains had parted and the girl who had been hiding behind them was coming towards him.

He looked at her and put his finger to his lips.

She stood still, motionless in the centre of the room, and waited.

Several seconds passed and at last the Marquis heard Sir Julius Stone's footsteps moving reluctantly down the corridor.

Only when he could hear them no longer did he move.

"He has . . . gone?" a soft voice asked.

"I think so," the Marquis answered, "but he could come back. You will have to be careful."

"Thank you . . . thank you . . . more than I can . . . express," the girl said in a breathless little voice.

"Come nearer to the fire," the Marquis suggested. "If you do not wish to encounter again your importunate admirer, I suggest you wait awhile before you return to your bed-room."

"I . . . cannot do . . . that," the girl said.

Once again the Marquis was aware of the terror in her face.

With a gesture of his hands he indicated a chair opposite to the one he intended to occupy and she sat down on the very edge of it, folding her shawl nervously across her breasts as if she suddenly realised how little she was wearing.

She looked very young and defenceless as she raised her eyes to the Marquis, and he smiled at her in a manner which unnumbered women had found beguiling and said quietly:

"Would you like to tell me why you are in this predicament?"

"I wish I . . . knew that . . . myself," she answered.

He seated himself opposite her, and as he was obviously waiting for her to go on she began to explain:

"I arrived here this evening with my maid on the Stage-coach. It had been arranged that the passengers should stay the night and we were given a meal all together in the main Dining-Room."

The Marquis knew that this was usual where an overnight stop was necessary. He was not particularly interested in what the girl was saying but in listening to the soft, musical tones of her voice.

He realised as he continued to look at her that she was even lovelier than he had at first thought.

In the light from the fire the colour of her hair reminded him of pictures by early Renaissance painters and he thought he had never seen a woman with such large eyes in a perfect oval face.

She had a small straight nose and her lips were exquisitely curved and were the soft pink of a blush-rose.

"What is your name?" he asked abruptly, breaking in on what she was about to say.

"Vanessa Lens," she replied.

"I am the Marquis of Ruckford. Now we are introduced!"

He thought her eyes widened a little in surprise and he said:

"You have perhaps heard of me?"

"Yes . . . I have heard that you own some very fine . . . paintings."

It was certainly not the answer the Marquis had expected.

"Do paintings interest you?" he asked.

"My father is a Miniaturist," she replied.

The Marquis thought for a moment.

"I have heard of Bernard Lens," he said, "but he lived much too long ago to be your father."

"Bernard Lens was my great-grandfather."

"That is very interesting!" the Marquis exclaimed. "I believe I am right in saying that he was the first English Artist to paint on ivory."

Vanessa's face lit up.

"It is nice to think you have heard of him. His work was very fine—and so is my father's."

"I hope that I shall have the pleasure of seeing some of it," the Marquis said.

"I hope so," Vanessa replied.

As if their exchange of conversation made her more vividly aware of the unconventional situation in which she found herself, she added nervously:

"Do you . . . think it would be . . . safe for me to go now?"

"I thought you said you could not go back to your bed-chamber," the Marquis answered.

"Not to the room I was in, but I could go upstairs to Dorcas, my maid. I would be safe with her until the morning . . . at least, I think so."

The doubt in her voice made the Marquis say:

"You have not yet finished telling me your story. Will you continue?"

"Yes . . . of course," Vanessa replied, "and then . . . perhaps you will . . . understand what has happened."

She drew in her breath, held her shawl a little tighter round her, and went on:

"I noticed the gentleman you called Stone come into the Dining-Room when we had nearly finished our meal. He was angry because the Landlord could not give him a private Parlour, but finally he sat down in the Dining-Room and ordered what he required with a bad grace. His table was opposite to where . . . I was sitting."

Vanessa's eyes were very expressive as she went on in a low voice:

"He kept staring at me. It was very . . . embarrassing, and then I saw him call a waiter."

She paused and the Marquis asked:

"What happened?"

"The waiter came to my side and asked if I would take a glass of wine with the gentleman. I refused, and Dorcas and I rose immediately to go upstairs to our rooms."

There was a little tremor in Vanessa's voice as she said:

"As we crossed the Dining-Room the gentleman also rose to his feet and stood in front of us.

" 'I think we have met before,' he said, 'and I shall be very hurt and distressed if you will not accept my hospitality.'

"'I am tired and wish to retire to bed, Sir,' I replied.

"'How can you be so ungracious?' he persisted. 'Just a glass of wine! I have many things I wish to say to you.'

"'Please, let me pass,' I said formally. 'I have already given you my answer.'

"'You are far too pretty to be so severe and puritanical,' he protested.

"As he was right in my path, I did not know what to do," Vanessa went on, "and then fortunately some of the other passengers in our party wished to leave and he was forced to stand aside."

"So you managed to avoid him," the Marquis said.

"Dorcas and I hurried upstairs," Vanessa went on. "We had been given two tiny attic-rooms at the very top of the Inn. All the people on the Stage-coach were housed up there."

"I am afraid that is their usual position," the Marquis smiled, "especially when the Inn is full!"

"We felt that the Landlord had little use for us when there were so many of the gentry to cater for," Vanessa said.

"Go on!" the Marquis ordered. "What happened next?"

"Dorcas was not feeling very well and I helped her into bed before I went to my own room," Vanessa continued. "She is old and she had no wish to come on the journey with me, but there was no-one else and I could not go alone."

"No, of course not," the Marquis agreed.

He thought how lovely she was in the firelight and found it not surprising that her looks should invite insults from men like Stone.

"I had gone to my own room and was just about to undress when there was a knock on the door," Vanessa went on. "I had naturally locked myself in, and I asked who was there. To my surprise, it was the Landlord!"

The Marquis raised his eye-brows but he did not speak.

"I asked him what he wanted. He was extremely

apologetic and told me that my particular room had been booked by someone else long before the Stage-coach arrived.

"He had taken a chance on the gentleman who had reserved it not turning up, but now he had done so, and it was very unfortunate, but I would have to change rooms."

Vanessa looked at the Marquis in consternation and added:

"It seems very . . . foolish of me now, but at the time I did not know what to do or what to say! While I was hesitating the Landlord picked up my valise and the clothes I had unpacked and started to walk down the stairs. There seemed to be nothing I could do but . . . follow him."

"Where did he take you?" the Marquis asked.

"To a room on this floor," Vanessa answered. "It was well furnished and obviously a much better room than the one I had just left. He put my things down and while I was still wondering what was happening he said:

" 'There will be no extra charge, Ma'am, and you will find this bed-chamber much more comfortable.'

"Of course, as soon as he had gone away I re-alised I should have asked him why he could not have put the gentleman who wanted my room in the one I was in now, but I was so slow-brained that I did not think of it until I was alone."

"I can understand your difficulty," the Marquis remarked.

"There was a fire in the new room and the bed was a large one," Vanessa said. "I just could not un-derstand why I should have been . . . moved."

"What did you do?" the Marquis asked.

"There seemed to be nothing I could do," Vanes-sa replied, "so I locked the door and undressed. I was just about to get into bed when I realised there was another door in the room.

"I had not noticed it at first, and then as I went towards it to make quite certain that it was locked . . . I heard a . . . voice on the other . . . side."

She paused and the Marquis saw that the fingers holding the shawl were trembling.

"I heard someone say, 'Thank you very much, my man!' and I knew who was speaking."

"It was undoubtedly Sir Julius Stone!" the Marquis said.

"Yes," Vanessa agreed, "and I was certain that he was responsible for having my room . . . changed!"

She drew in her breath as if she remembered the terror of it and went on:

"I stood wondering what I should do. I looked at the communicating door and realised that there was no key on my side! Then I heard the click in the lock as the key was . . . turned."

There was an echo of the fear the Marquis had seen in her eyes as Vanessa said:

"I realised then what was . . . happening, and running across the bed-room I opened the door onto the passage. As I went I knew . . . he was not far . . . behind me!

"I saw a man coming out of this room and I thought it must be empty. I opened the door and looked inside. . . . Seeing no-one, I . . . thought I could . . . lock myself . . . in."

Vanessa's voice was breathless as she finished speaking.

"I think you were very sensible," the Marquis said quietly. "Only someone like Stone would behave in such a despicable manner to a girl travelling alone with only an old maid-servant to accompany her."

Vanessa did not speak and after a moment he said:

"You would be completely safe nine times out of ten, but there is always the tenth! Was your journey of such importance that there was no-one more responsible to go with you?"

"No . . . no-one," she answered. "Lord Derwent had asked my father to bring him six miniatures he had recently restored. His Lordship also said he had some others in his house about which he would appreciate my father's advice."

"But your father could not do as Lord Derwent requested?" the Marquis questioned.

"It was impossible," Vanessa said with a little gesture of one hand. "He has been ill . . . very ill! So I thought if I took the miniatures to Lord Derwent I could also tell him which of the others in his collection were in need of attention."

"You are an expert?" the Marquis asked with a faintly derisive smile.

"I have helped my father for a long time," Vanessa replied with dignity.

"I apologise for suggesting you were not capable," the Marquis said. "But you look very like a miniature yourself. It is hard to think of you working as an Artist, or maybe that is my mistake—perhaps that sort of painting comes naturally to you."

"I do not presume to call myself a Miniaturist," Vanessa said reprovingly, "but I am experienced enough to know what should be done to a miniature which has faded or which has been affected by the temperature."

The Marquis did not speak and after a moment she said as if she challenged his knowledge of such matters:

"The whole difficulty with painting on ivory is that it may warp or produce a mildew which can ruin the painting."

"I am aware of that," the Marquis replied. "So you were able to advise Lord Derwent?"

"I found there were four miniatures which needed restoration," Vanessa answered.

"I hope His Lordship was grateful to you for bringing him the others at such a risk to yourself."

"I do not think His Lordship thought about it! But if an owner receives a completed order personally, he normally pays the bill on the spot."

She gave the Marquis a shy smile and added:

"That is something which is too often forgotten by those who do not have to work for their living."

"That is true," the Marquis agreed, thinking of the huge pile of debts accumulated by the Prince of

Wales, many of which were owed to Artists or Dealers.

There was silence and then Vanessa said:

"Do you . . . think it is . . . safe now for me to go . . . upstairs?"

The Marquis was watching her sensitive little face, and the mere idea of her being in close proximity to a man as depraved as Sir Julius Stone made him feel angry.

"Why could the swine not keep his leching and whoring to London?" he asked himself.

It was unfortunate that this inexperienced child should have met someone like him at a Posting-Inn.

The Marquis guessed that the reason for Sir Julius's appearance was that he had attended the Mill.

"When I travel," he said slowly after a moment, "because I dislike noise, I always engage not only the bed-room in which I sleep, but also the rooms on either side of it. This ensures that I am not kept awake by snoring or quarrelling in the adjoining rooms! The walls are often remarkably thin."

"It sounds very luxurious," Vanessa said with a smile.

"Comfort is something which I believe is worth paying for," the Marquis replied loftily. "What I am suggesting, Miss Lens, is that you should sleep in the room next to mine. This will ensure that Sir Julius will not molest you, and as you doubtless are leaving early in the morning, you will be away long before he is awake."

"Can I really do that?" Vanessa asked.

"I think it is a sensible solution," the Marquis replied.

He rose from the chair by the fireside as he spoke and walked across the room.

The communicating door was situated between two large wardrobes and the key was on his side. He turned it and then, lifting a candlestick from an adjacent table, walked into the next room.

It was much smaller than the one he was using

and had obviously been intended for use as a dressing-room or for a child whose parents occupied the double room.

There was a small, narrow bed in one corner, a wardrobe, and a chest, all of good quality, and there was a carpet on the floor.

"This will suit me perfectly!" Vanessa exclaimed. "In the morning I can go upstairs to Dorcas and she can fetch my clothes from the other bed-room."

The Marquis put the candlestick he was carrying down on a bedside table.

"I suggest we transfer the key from my side of the door to yours," he said.

He looked at Vanessa as he spoke.

"I trust you," she said in a low voice. "You are very . . . different from that . . . horrible man."

"I should hope so!" the Marquis answered dryly.

"Papa told me that there were men . . . like him, and that the Prince of Wales accepts them," Vanessa said almost as if she was speaking to herself. "But I never thought to meet . . . one."

"And now that you have done so, you realise how careful you must be!" the Marquis said. "You are very lovely, Vanessa, and lovely women often quite unconsciously court danger."

She looked at him in surprise.

"Do you mean that?" she asked.

"Of course I mean it," the Marquis answered. "Surely you must look in your mirror?"

The colour rose in her cheeks and she gave him a shy little smile.

"My mother was beautiful," she said, "so I suppose I have never thought of myself as being anything but . . . very ordinary."

"Which is something a great many men will try to persuade you you are not!" the Marquis said.

"Then it is perhaps fortunate for me that I do not meet many," Vanessa replied.

She smiled at him again and he looked down at her.

She looked very small and insubstantial in the candlelight. She seemed in fact little more than a child with her attractive hair framing her face. It seemed to gleam against the shadows of the room.

"While your father is ill and unable to look after you, you must stay at home, Vanessa," the Marquis said in his deep voice. "You must never again be reckless and go off on journeys such as this without your maid to chaperon you."

"I am sure you are . . . right," Vanessa replied slowly, "but it is . . . difficult . . . very . . . difficult."

There was a worried note in her voice which seemed to the Marquis somehow pathetic.

"Go to sleep," he said after a moment, "and for tonight do not be afraid of anything. Lock both the doors in this room and if you are frightened you can cry out and I shall hear you."

"I am sure I shall be safe now . . . thanks to you, My Lord," she said softly. "I am grateful . . . more grateful than I can . . . say."

"There is no need for you to thank me," the Marquis said. "I am only sorry that this should have happened, but perhaps it will make you a little more careful in the future."

"Another time . . . you might not be . . . there."

Her eyes met his and suddenly it seemed in some strange manner as if they were, both of them, very still.

She looked unreal, almost a figment of the imagination as she stood looking up at him, her grey-green eyes a little bewildered and yet trusting, her lips just parted.

"Good-night!" the Marquis said, and the words seemed hardly to disturb the air between them.

Then as if he could not help himself he put his finger under her chin, bent his head, and his lips touched hers.

It was a very gentle, passionless kiss; the kiss a man might have given to a child. Yet as their lips were held by each other's it was impossible to move or breathe.

The Marquis raised his head.

"Good-night, Vanessa!" he said again.

Now his voice sounded abrupt and loud, and

without looking at her he walked through the communicating door and passed into his own room.

He heard the door close behind him and the key turn in the lock.

Then he walked slowly to the arm-chair by the fireside to sit down in it, staring into the flames.

Chapter Two

The Marquis of Ruckford entered Carlton House appreciating as he did so the dignity of the facade with its fine Corinthian portico.

Every time he visited the Prince of Wales he could not help being pleased artistically not only with the outward appearance of Carlton House, which Holland had altered out of all recognition, but also with the interior.

The Prince's servants in their dark blue uniforms trimmed elaborately with gold lace led him through the splendid Hall with Ionic columns of brown Sienna marble and up the graceful double staircase to the State Apartments.

The Marquis passed through the Music-Room towards the Drawing-Room decorated with Chinese furniture and hangings. It was a taste which had been cultivated by many admirers in England since the 1750s.

As he walked slowly and with dignity he looked extremely elegant in his well-fitting clothes which were all the more impressive because, unlike those of so many Beaux or Dandies, they were not in the least flamboyant.

It was true that the Marquis had followed the dictates of Beau Brummel, who had decreed that a gentleman should be so perfectly attired that he was in fact unnoticeable.

It would, however, have been impossible not to notice the Marquis. There was something about him which commanded attention and, accustomed as they were to an amazing variety of visitors, the Palace servants glanced at him appreciatively.

The footmen looked with envy at his broad shoulders, knowing that he could, if he wished, floor even a professional pugilist, and had in fact done so on several occasions.

The Marquis, quite unaware of the interest he aroused, was looking at the pictures and furniture and realised that some of them were unknown to him. He remembered that Lady Sarah Spencer had said to him:

"The Prince changes the furniture so very often that one can scarcely find time to catch a glimpse at each transient arrangement before it is all turned out for some other."

The magnificent Van Dycks which the Prince had recently acquired were, however, well known to the Marquis, as were the Dutch landscapes which His Royal Highness had bought despite the fact that the Dutch painters were not at the moment fashionable.

The furniture was in the Marquis's eyes peerless; for the Prince after the Revolution had purchased treasures which were being disposed of with incredible stupidity from Versailles and the other great houses of France.

In fact, there was no doubt that the Prince had the most comprehensive collection of French works of Art ever assembled by an English Monarch.

When they reached the Chinese Drawing-Room the flunkey announced the Marquis without first asking his name, since he was in fact so well known at Carlton House.

"The Marquis of Ruckford, Your Royal Highness!" he intoned rather in the manner of an Archbishop speaking from the Pulpit.

The Prince, who was alone and was staring at some sketches of the Royal Pavilion at Brighton, rose to his feet.

"Ruckford! I had no idea that you had returned to London! I am delighted to see you, my dear boy. What are the results of your journey?"

"That is what I have come to relate to you, Sire," the Marquis replied.

"Sit down! Sit down!" the Prince suggested, "and have a glass of wine."

As if it was anticipated that this would be required, the Butler, assisted by two footmen, carried into the room a large silver tray on which there were several heavy cut-glass decanters and some crystal glasses engraved with the Royal Insignia.

The Marquis accepted a glass of wine; the Prince chose brandy.

"Did you buy me the Titian?" the Prince asked as the servants' task was completed.

He spoke with the enthusiasm of a young boy who has been promised a treat and can no longer wait to hear if he is to be allowed to enjoy it.

The Marquis shook his head.

"I am afraid not, Sire. Lord Hargrave was somewhat chagrined when I was obliged to inform him that the picture was in fact a copy."

The Prince laughed.

"I am sure Hargrave was infuriated. He spoke to me in such glowing terms of the painting and was quite certain I would wish to buy it."

"It is something I would advise you not to do, Sire."

"You know as well as I do that I shall take your advice," the Prince said. "A copy!"

He laughed again.

"I wish I had seen Hargrave's expression when you told him so."

"He was slightly mollified, Sire, by the fact that I found a very fine Jan Van Goyen hanging in a passage where no-one had noticed it for years."

"Van Goyen!"

The Prince's eyes were shining.

"You bought it for me?"

"I did, Sire. It will go well with your collection of Dutch paintings."

"What is it like? Describe it to me!" the Prince commanded.

"It is a particularly picturesque view of the Dutch countryside. The moisture-laden atmosphere and the looming grey sky reflected in the canal is in Van Goyen's inimitable manner."

"I cannot wait to see it!" the Prince said with a sigh of satisfaction. "You have brought it with you?"

"I have it at Ruckford House, Sire, but I would like, if you will allow me to do so, to have it cleaned and reframed before I bring it to you."

"That is very good of you, Ruckford," the Prince said. "So there was nothing else in Hargrave's collection that I would have liked?"

"There was a Rubens, Sire, but I bought that for myself."

"You did what?" the Prince exclaimed.

"I bought it for Ruckford Park. It is just what I needed in the State Dining-Room."

The Prince was frowning.

"I think if you have found such a treasure, Ruckford, since I had sent you to Hargrave Castle on my behalf, the picture should be mine!"

The Prince sounded rather like a greedy child and the Marquis smiled as he answered:

"I think, Sire, the labourer is worthy of his hire, and this particular picture in size and colour is exactly what I have been looking for, for some time."

The Prince glared at him, then suddenly his expression cleared and he laughed.

"Damn you, Ruckford, you are always the same! If you see something you want, you take it! You are a pirate—that is what you are!"

"My ancestor, the first Ruckford, Sire, was Knighted by Queen Elizabeth for his thieving ways."

"But he was stealing from the Spaniards!" the Prince remarked.

"Once a pirate—always a pirate, Sire!" the Mar-

quis said lightly. "And you must remember you in-
structed me to buy you a Titian, not a Rubens."

"You are splitting straws," the Prince said accus-
ingly. "At the same time, I am well aware that I cannot prevent you from cheating me."

"That is a hard word, Sire," the Marquis protested. "Perhaps I should have told you in the first
place that Lord Hargrave insisted before a picture
even leaves the Castle that he should receive the
money for it."

There was silence.

"Does that mean I cannot have the Van Goyen?"
the Prince asked in a different voice.

"I told you, Sire, that I have brought it with me,"
the Marquis answered. "I have paid for it, but it is
yours!"

"I will repay you, Ruckford, you know that," the
Prince said. "But you also know it is almost impossible
for me to find any money at this particular moment."

"That is why I was quite certain, Sire, that you
would not grudge me the Rubens for which His Lordship asked quite a considerable sum."

The Marquis was well aware that His Royal
Highness owed large sums already to a number of
Artists. Gainsborough's widow had received only a
portion of the sum outstanding when her husband
died.

Cosway was owed nearly two thousand pounds
and Stubbs over a thousand. There were others, like
Hoppner and George Romney, to whom the Prince
was permanently in debt.

But these were footling sums compared with
those owed elsewhere. The bill of Leeders, the coach-
builders, was over £32,000, and the Prince's various
tailors—Weston, Schweitzer, Bazalgette, and Winter
—were owed between them £31,919.

He was in debt to his friends—more than
£15,000 to the Earl of Morre—while members of the
Royal Household had not been paid for months.

As if the Prince was well aware of where his
thoughts and those of the Marquis were centred, he
changed the subject.

"I have some more acquisitions to show you," he said eagerly. "I will say one thing for you, Ruckford, there is no-one else who appreciates my purchases as you do."

"Thank you, Sire," the Marquis replied. "I think the truth is that we have the same taste in many things. For instance, we both appreciate French furniture and Flemish paintings. Your Royal Highness has an unerring eye which has proved itself over and over again, and I would like to think that I am not often deceived where the genuine article is concerned."

"No, indeed, you have the eye of a connoisseur," the Prince agreed generously.

It was obvious that he was delighted at the compliment his friend had paid him.

"There is one thing I would like to ask you about, Sire," the Marquis said. "Have you ever heard of a Miniaturist called Lens? I do not mean Bernard Lens, of course, who has been dead for many years."

"Is the Lens in whom you are interested some relation of his?" the Prince asked.

"His grandson."

"Then you must mean Cornelius Lens," the Prince replied. "I have one of his miniatures, and two or perhaps three years ago he restored one of my Hilliards which had faded in the sunshine."

"Does he do a lot of restorative work?" the Marquis asked.

"He was recommended to me because Cosway has grown too big for his boots when it comes to restoring a miniature he has not painted himself."

"And you found Lens good?" the Marquis enquired.

"Exceptionally!" the Prince said. "If you are interested, I will show you what he did for me."

"I am interested," the Marquis replied.

The Prince led the way from the Chinese Room through the Golden Drawing-Room and the Rose-Satin Drawing-Room to the Blue-Velvet Room.

Here arranged on either side of a magnificently carved chimney piece were a number of miniatures.

The Marquis remembered having seen them before but in a different setting. Against blue damask walls they were extremely decorative and the Prince pointed out a magnificent Hans Holbein with small pearls hanging from a frame, and two Nicholas Hilliards, one of Queen Elizabeth and one of Sir Walter Raleigh, whose workmanship was superb.

The paintings on vellum showed all the extravagance and splendour of the Elizabethan age and the gold embroidery and fine lace ruffs gave plenty of scope for the Artist's exceptional talents.

"Did you know," the Prince asked with a smile, "that Hilliard's admonition to a painter was not to get angry while he was working, but to shut out questioners and busy-bodies."

"That is something we would all like to do, Sire," the Marquis said with a smile.

"Even Cosway cannot equal the brilliance of the early Miniaturists," the Prince said.

As he spoke he picked up a miniature of Mrs. Fitzherbert which was hanging amongst the others.

The Prince had bought no less than thirty pictures from Richard Cosway, who had been appointed Miniaturist to His Royal Highness at the end of the last century.

He had in fact become a great friend of the Prince, but the Marquis had never liked him. He was a conceited, cocky little man who adopted the more ostentatious mode of dress of the Dandies.

He carried this to such an extreme that the cartoonists called him the "Marconi Miniature Painter" and the name stuck.

The self-styled "Marconis" were the younger members of the Almanack Club and were noted for their absurd and extravagant ideas.

Cosway's foppish attire, and in particular his habit of wearing a sword on all occasions, layed him wide open to ridicule.

At the same time, there was no doubt that he was an extremely clever and proficient painter, although there were many unfavourable stories told about him.

Before the Prince of Wales came under the good

influence of Maria Fitzherbert he had spent much of his time with John Philip Turnbull, the brother of Sarah Siddons, the actress, who was reported to swallow wine by "pailfuls" and with Richard Cosway was said to have "turned his house into a brothel."

They were only two of the number of undesirables whom the Prince had received as close friends, and who encouraged him to drink to excess to squander money and incur ever greater debts.

Maria Fitzherbert fortunately had been a restraining and beneficent influence on the Prince's life, and thinking of her now, the Marquis remembered that His Royal Highness had given Mrs. Fitzherbert a large diamond which she had cut in two.

Cosway had painted her miniature and also painted one of the Prince, which they had set into two small lockets, each covered with one half of the large diamond encircled by smaller ones.

The Prince and Mrs. Fitzherbert had vowed that they would always wear the lockets, and the Marquis had heard the Prince say on various occasions that on his death her portrait should be interred with him.

At the same time, the Marquis did not like Cosway, however good a painter he might be, and had no great partiality for Artists as a race.

"Ah!" the Prince exclaimed suddenly. "This is what I am looking for."

He took down a miniature from the wall and handed it to the Marquis.

"That was painted by Cornelius Lens," he said. "I bought it several years ago."

The Marquis took it in his hands and saw at once that it was a portrait of Vanessa.

He recognised immediately that the workmanship was not only very fine but that the Artist had painted the miniature with love.

Lens had portrayed not only the perfect oval of Vanessa's face and the appeal in her large grey-green eyes; he had also captured a look of spirituality about her which the Marquis could not find in any of the other portraits hanging on the wall.

He guessed that the miniature had been painted when Vanessa was about fifteen or sixteen years old.

Yet she had seemed very little more mature when he had rescued her from the odious advances of Sir Julius Stone and kissed her good-night before she locked the door of their adjoining rooms.

The strange beauty of her fair hair touched with gold was as ably portrayed as the hair of the Madonna in a miniature by Hans Memling, which the Prince also possessed.

The Marquis realised that the Prince was waiting for his comments and he said:

"I like the miniature, Sire, and I wish to get in touch with the Artist."

"If you are going to call on Cornelius Lens," the Prince replied, "then perhaps you would take with you that miniature of James I by Isaac Oliver. As you see, it is in need of restoration and I had in fact meant to send for Lens to attend to it."

"I will take it to him, Sire," the Marquis said.

He was well aware that the Prince could always find an errand for any of his friends, and with a faint smile on his lips he lifted down from the wall the portrait of James I resplendent in embroidered doublet with a lace-trimmed ruff.

"Ask him not to take too long about it," the Prince admonished, "although I dare say I have a miniature stored away somewhere which can fill up the gap on the wall."

The Marquis was quite sure of that, knowing how much the Prince accumulated; a great deal of which was not on show because there was no room.

"How shall I find Cornelius Lens's address?" he enquired.

"John McMahon will have it somewhere," the Prince replied casually.

As John McMahon had just become Keeper of the Privy Purse, the Marquis thought with a wry smile that his first job would have been to compile a list of debts that the Prince still owed.

He wondered if Cornelius Lens had been paid for his services.

He had, however, found out all he wished to know, and on the Prince's insistence he stayed to dine at Carlton House with a party which included not only Mrs. Fitzherbert but also the beautiful Duchess of Devonshire. He decided that on the following day he would visit Vanessa's father.

There was a large number of family miniatures at Ruckford House in Berkeley Square.

All down the centuries the Ruckfords had patronised the Arts and had their portraits painted for posterity by the leading Artists of the day.

The Marquis had found that he owned several Isaac Olivers, as did the Prince; also a number of Samual Coopers painted in the reign of Charles II, when he had portrayed many of the notorious Restoration beauties.

Besides these, Cooper had immortalised the first Countess of Ruckford, a great beauty of her day who was reputed to have been one of the few virtuous ladies to refuse the favours of the King.

There was no doubt that her portrait required attention, and having had it carefully parcelled up with the other miniature, the Marquis set off in his phaeton for Islington.

John McMahon had told him where Cornelius Lens lived.

"At least, I hope he is still there, M'Lord," John McMahon had added. "You know what these Artists are like. They wander from place to place and often forget to leave an address behind them. I had great difficulty in finding a glazier the other day whom His Highness required urgently."

The Marquis paid little attention to the complaints of the Keeper of the Privy Purse. He only hoped that Cornelius Lens would not have moved, because he was anxious to see Vanessa.

He really wished to convince himself that she was as lovely as he remembered; that the originality he had sensed in her had not been a trick of the candlelight.

He had gone to sleep expecting to see her next

morning; but when his valet called him he learnt that the first Stage-coach had departed from the Posting-Inn at a half after six o'clock and Vanessa and her maid had been on it.

He felt certain that in that case she would not have encountered Sir Julius Stone before she left.

The Marquis caught a glimpse of that gentleman as he left the private Parlour in which he had break-fasted, and noted with satisfaction that the Baronet was looking surly and clearly frustrated!

The thought added to his own good humour as he set off to tool his horses so expertly that he did in fact beat Lord Derwent's record, much to the admiration of his staff.

"We have seldom had a better team, Higham," the Marquis said to his coachman when he arrived back at Berkeley Square.

"That's just what I thought myself, M'Lord," Higham replied. "But it makes a difference who's a-driving them!"

"You flatter me!" the Marquis said with a laugh as he walked into his house.

Situated on one side of the Square, Ruckford House surrounded by its own walled garden, was not only a large and impressive Mansion, it was also as full of treasures as the Prince's aspiring Palace in Pall Mall.

This, however, was the product not only of the present owner's good taste but also the fact that all down the ages the Ruckfords had been collectors or, as the Prince liked to call them—"pirates."

The Marquis would often laughingly refer to his family motto, which when translated from the Latin read: "What I have, I hold."

It was certainly what the Ruckfords had done!

They had, together with their possessions, sur-vived the Civil War and the ravages of Cromwell's Army, the depressions in the various centuries which had annihilated many other rich families, and had managed, through a cleverness all their own, always to remain on the right side of the Monarch in power.

The Marquis's vast possessions in Oxfordshire

were unparalleled, and if Ruckford House in Berkeley Square was a collector's dream, it was nothing compared with the beauty and importance of Ruckford Park.

As he drove towards Islington the Marquis could not help thinking how fortunate he was to find treasures wherever he might be.

"I have a nose for them," he told himself.

He was, as it happened, particularly delighted with the Rubens he had bought from Lord Hargrave.

It was not typical of Rubens's usual pictures of large, fleshy beauties whom he personally admired, or even an allegorical orgy of gods and goddesses.

It was in fact an exquisite landscape with the sun sinking behind a fairy-like Château surrounded by a lake.

It was not what one expected of Rubens and yet to the Marquis it had a mystical charm of its own.

He thought that in a way it had the same kind of charm Vanessa had.

Finding her had been like discovering the first white violet of the spring under a profusion of leaves, or seeing a snow-drop valiantly defying the snow, perfect in its purity.

"Nevertheless, I expect to be disappointed," the Marquis told himself.

In the past he had often in the evening met a woman at a Ball, or seen an actress on the stage, who had made him feel here was something unusual and he must pursue it.

He could not explain to himself the feeling he had, and yet it was very much the same as when he saw a picture which he was certain must be a masterpiece perhaps hidden under layers of dust and dirt, or when he came suddenly upon a breathtaking view when he was driving or riding and thinking of other things.

Just for a moment there would be a sort of physical jerk to his heart which would engender a strange breathlessness, as if he stood on the threshold of a sanctuary.

It was a feeling as exquisite and as poignant as

the rising of a physical desire. But like desire, all too soon he would find that he was mistaken and there would be only the aftermath of disappointment.

When this happened the Marquis laughed at himself.

Why should he expect it to be otherwise? Why should he always imagine that he could capture perfection when other men had spent a lifetime trying to do that very thing and failed utterly?

At the same time, it was something he could not help, and there was always the hope that one day he would find what he sought, whatever it might be, and not be disappointed.

It was, however, with a cynical twist of his lips that the Marquis, having driven most expertly through streets crowded with drays, gilded carriages of the aristocracy, droves of oxen, coal wagons, and blaspheming draymen, reached the comparative quiet of Islington.

Here the trees in the Square wore the bright green of spring and the daffodils were golden yellow in the front gardens.

The house that the Marquis sought was standing by itself behind the more formal, balconied buildings in the Square and was in fact little more than a cottage.

It was surrounded by a wall which enclosed a very small garden and at first sight the Marquis thought it looked rather like a child's toy; a dolls'-house from which all adults should be excluded.

At a second glance he was, however, certain that at one time it must have been built for an Artist. As it faced south, undoubtedly at the back there would be a studio with a north light.

The groom jumped down from the phaeton and, passing through a small iron gate, rapped at a green-painted door with a knocker which gleamed brightly in the sunshine.

It was a while before the door opened and an elderly woman stood there.

The Marquis guessed that this was Dorcas, who had accompanied Vanessa on her journey to Lord

Derwent's house and who looked, he thought, exactly the sort of respectable, well-trained servant that Vanessa should have in her employment.

The groom came back to the phaeton and the Marquis climbed down.

"Good-morning!" he said to the maid. "I wish to speak with Mr. Cornelius Lens."

The old woman looked him over with speculative eyes which in other circumstances the Marquis would have thought impertinent, but he had the feeling that she was perhaps afraid that he might be Sir Julius Stone and said quickly:

"I am the Marquis of Ruckford, and I have come to see Mr. Lens on business."

He was almost certain that the maid-servant relaxed her scrutiny. At any rate, she stood a little aside and said:

"Will you come in, M'Lord? I'll tell Miss Vanessa you're here."

The Hall of the house was so small that the Marquis felt unnaturally large as he set his hat down on a narrow oak table and followed the maid as she opened the door of a Sitting-Room.

The window looked on to the front of the house and through it he could see his phaeton moving away as his groom walked the horses so that they would not become restless.

Looking round the small room, he saw that it was furnished in good taste, although the furniture was not expensive.

There was, however, over the chimneypiece a superb picture of an exceptionally lovely woman. The likeness to Vanessa was very striking, and he was sure it must be her mother.

She was undoubtedly a lady of breeding, which was somehow reassuring; for the Marquis was still expecting to be disappointed when he saw Vanessa herself.

He could not explain why he thought, or rather felt, that she was different from other young women he had met. Certainly a great gulf yawned between her and the families of artistic people he had known in the past.

It was not only Richard Cosway who had disgusted him with the way in which he pandered to the Prince in the years when he drank so heavily that after several days of it he would be obliged to take to his bed with a high fever.

He was frequently drunk in the company of Richard Brinsley Sheridan, who, while having achieved international fame with his plays *The Rivals*, *School for Scandal*, and *The Critic*, was not the type of young man to be called a steadying influence.

The Prince's other friends were remarkably varied and, while they were never fools and some of them were brilliantly clever, they certainly did not improve the Prince's image where the public was concerned.

Yet the Prince also had many more balanced friends like the Marquis, who found his company delightful.

He was a brilliant conversationalist, and had as the Duke of Wellington said, "a most extraordinary talent for imitating the manner, gestures, and even the voice of other people."

George Brummel thought his "power of mimicry was so extraordinary that if his lot had fallen that way, he would have been the best comic actor in Europe."

The Prince had grace, wit, and was an excellent critic of music.

But because he had seen at close quarters how easily the Prince could damage his public image and waste his talents with undesirable associates, the Marquis was particularly careful where his own reputation was concerned.

He had no intention of being laughed at in the Clubs or sneered at in Mayfair Drawing-Rooms.

He was proud of his antecedents and he was far too self-controlled to indulge himself in a way which would cause tongues to wag or could affect his health.

He enjoyed good living; but he had made up his mind when he was still young that he would never indulge to excess, and that was a rule to which he had kept rigidly all through the years.

He was staring at the portrait over the chimney-piece when the door behind him opened.

He turned round and saw, as he had expected, that it was Vanessa.

For a moment he looked at her and as her eyes met his he saw the colour rise in her fair skin.

It was almost like watching the dawn creeping up the sky, and he knew in that moment that she was even more lovely then he remembered.

Small, petite, her face identical to the miniature the Prince had shown him, there was still that strange, untouched spirituality about her which he had remembered so vividly even though he thought he would have found it hard in retrospect to describe her features.

But her little nose was straight, her lips exquisitely curved, and he knew that never in his lifetime had he seen eyes that were so large or so expressive.

Vanessa curtseyed and he knew that for the first few moments when she looked at him it had been impossible for her to remember her manners.

"Good-morning, Vanessa!" the Marquis said in his deep voice. "Are you surprised to see me?"

"Yes . . ." Vanessa answered, little above a whisper. "I could not . . . believe it was true when Dorcas said . . . you were here. . . ."

"It was not difficult for me to find you," the Marquis replied. "I had only to ask the Prince of Wales for your address. He had bought a miniature painted by your father. It was an excellent portrait of you."

"My father did not . . . say who it was," Vanessa answered. "It was entitled *Portrait of an Unknown Girl*."

"You could hardly expect me not to recognise it," the Marquis said.

She had not looked at him since the first moment she had come into the room and the Marquis knew that she was very shy.

Now with an effort she came forward and said with a gesture of her hand:

"Will you not sit down, My Lord?"

He noticed that her fingers were long and perfectly shaped and remembered how she had clutched her white shawl across her breasts when she had sat on the edge of the chair in his bed-room.

"I thought perhaps I could see your father," the Marquis said. "I have a message for him from the Prince."

Vanessa did not answer and he said after a moment:

"Do not feel embarrassed if the studio is untidy. I am used to Artists and know that they dislike having to compose themselves to receive visitors."

"I am afraid it is . . . impossible for you to meet my father, My Lord," Vanessa said in a low voice. "He has been ill . . . very ill . . . as I told you."

She paused for a moment and added:

"The Doctor has forbidden him to have . . . visitors of any sort . . . but of course I can take him a message."

The Marquis sat down on a small sofa and drew from his pocket the two miniatures he had brought with him.

"I have here a commission from His Royal Highness," he said. "He asks that your father will restore as quickly as possible the miniature of James I by Isaac Oliver. As you see, it has faded."

He took it from the soft leather wrapping in which his secretary had enclosed it and handed it to Vanessa.

She gave a little sigh.

"Why will people be so stupid as to leave miniatures in the sunlight?" she asked. "It is too strong for the delicacy of the painting."

"I am afraid I must plead guilty to the same crime," the Marquis said. "I have brought you a miniature of my ancestress Mary, Countess of Ruckford, painted by Cooper. That also has faded."

"How pretty she is!" Vanessa exclaimed. "And how exciting it will be to see her as the Artist painted her. You see how the blue of her gown has gone almost grey? Her eyes have faded too."

"I am sure I can leave it in your father's capable hands," the Marquis said. "Now tell me about yourself."

He thought that Vanessa looked at him a little nervously.

"What does Your Lordship wish to know?" she asked.

"There are quite a lot of things about which I am curious," the Marquis replied. "Of what does your family consist? I imagine that is a picture of your mother over the mantelshelf?"

"Mama died three years ago," Vanessa replied. "She found the fogs and cold of the winter very trying. The Doctor said she should go to a warmer climate, but it was . . . something which we could not . . . afford."

"You are poor?" the Marquis enquired.

"We have . . . only what Papa . . . makes."

"But your great-grandfather must have been a rich man. I was recalling what I knew about him," the Marquis said. "He was in great demand as a teacher and had many important pupils—amongst them George I and George II."

"Yes, I know," Vanessa answered, "but while Artists may make a lot of money one year, they spend it the next, and great-grandpapa had two sons, the second being my grandfather, Peter Paul Lens."

"What did he do?" the Marquis enquired.

"He was also a Miniaturist but not a very famous one. There is very little of his work to be seen."

She paused and then she said:

"He was also very wild and . . . irresponsible."

"He sounds like one of my ancestors," the Marquis smiled.

"Grandpapa played a leading part in a Hellfire Club which was called the 'Blasters' in Dublin in 1737. All his friends were very disorderly and he made no secret of the fact that he was a disciple of the devil and drank to him publicly."

"He sounds very disreputable," the Marquis agreed.

"He behaved so badly," Vanessa went on, "that

his behaviour was censured by the Irish House of Lords and he had to leave the country and return to England."

"Did he continue to paint miniatures?" the Marquis enquired.

"For a little while. He married, Papa was born, and then he died when he was only thirty-five."

"It sounds a very Miniaturist sort of life!" the Marquis remarked.

"It meant that Papa had to work his own way in the world," Vanessa said. "Luckily he could teach, like his grandfather, and he painted so well that he sold his miniatures almost as soon as he completed them."

Vanessa paused.

"Go on!" the Marquis prompted.

"He had a number of commissions to paint whole families and it was while he was painting my mother that he fell in love with her."

The Marquis glanced up at the picture over the chimneypiece.

"I can understand that," he said. "She must have been very beautiful, and you are very like her, Vanessa."

"As I told you the night we met," Vanessa said, "I could never be as lovely as Mama. She was so happy and gay and she loved Papa so deeply that no picture could do her justice."

"I can understand your feeling like that," the Marquis said.

His eyes were not on the picture but on Vanessa's face as she looked up at it and on the long line of her white neck as it ended in her little round chin.

"Please continue," he begged.

"Mama was betrothed to a gentleman who was rich. Her father did not approve of Artists and especially Papa, who was much older than she was. When Mama told my grandfather that she wished to marry Papa he was furious and threw him out of the house."

"I can guess what happened," the Marquis smiled.

"Mama ran away with him and her family never

spoke to her again. It upset Papa to think about it and so it is something we have never discussed."

"But they were happy?" the Marquis asked.

"So very . . . very happy," Vanessa replied. "The house seems empty without Mama, and poor Papa was so lost . . ."

She made a little gesture with her hand which was very eloquent.

There was a silence. Then the Marquis asked:

"Do you never go to parties?"

"We have very few friends in London," Vanessa answered. "Mama did not like the . . . artistic world."

"I can understand that," the Marquis said, thinking of Richard Cosway. "But now that your mother is not here and your father is ill, you must lead a very lonely existence."

"I have Dorcas," Vanessa replied, then added: "and of course, because Papa is ill, I . . . help him with his . . . work."

The Marquis hesitated, as if he was choosing his words with care.

"I wonder if your father would allow you to come driving with me one afternoon? I am sure that you appreciate fine horse-flesh, and my chestnuts beat the record on the return journey to London yesterday!"

"How exciting!" Vanessa exclaimed. "I love horses. I used to ride when we lived in the country."

She paused before she added:

"But Papa did not get enough commissions when we were away from London, and so we had to live here."

"I will lend you a horse if you wish to ride," the Marquis said.

He saw the sudden light in her eyes before she replied:

"I do not think that it would be . . . correct for me to accept such an offer from you, My Lord . . . would it?"

It was the question of a child asking for guidance and the Marquis hesitated before he answered:

"I think in the circumstances it would be quite

permissible for you to do so, and anyway who would know?"

"Perhaps I should . . . consider your kind offer," Vanessa said, "and thank you very much for . . . thinking of it."

The Marquis had a feeling that when Vanessa thought it over she would refuse and he said insistently:

"But you will allow me to take you driving? After all, even the most closely chaperoned young women are permitted to drive in Hyde Park."

"Thank you," Vanessa answered. "I would like that very much!"

"Then I will call for you tomorrow," the Marquis said, "at about two o'clock. Will you be ready for me?"

"I shall be ready," Vanessa answered. "But you are quite certain, My Lord, it will not be an imposition and will not . . . bore you?"

"I assure you," the Marquis replied, "I never allow myself to be bored; and I have a fancy, Vanessa, that there are many things for us to talk about."

"I cannot think what those can be," she answered, "except of course pictures. I do know a little about Art, but not half as much as you do."

"I will tell you about the pictures I have in London and at my house in the country," the Marquis promised.

"I would also like to be told about those owned by the Prince of Wales," Vanessa said. "Are they really breathtakingly wonderful?"

"I am sure you would think so," the Marquis replied.

"I would like to see his Greuzes," Vanessa said. "I think the delicacy of his painting and the liquid expression that he captures in the eyes are more lifelike than those executed by any other painter."

"He should have painted you," the Marquis said. "Your eyes, Vanessa, are very expressive. Someone once said that eyes mirror the soul. In your case they were speaking the truth."

Vanessa blushed. Then she said:

"It is . . . embarrassing to think that people might be able to know my . . . secrets by looking into my . . . eyes."

"Do you not think that is true of everyone?" the Marquis asked. "If you look into a man's eyes you can tell if he is honest, and . . ."

He was going to add: "if you look into a woman's you will know if she is in love," and then he felt that that was not the sort of remark he should make to Vanessa.

Instead he said:

"I have always been told that if you look a lion or a tiger straight in the eyes the animal will not spring at you."

"I am not prepared to put it to the test!" Vanessa exclaimed and they both laughed.

Reluctantly the Marquis rose to his feet.

"I will leave you until tomorrow," he said, "and in the meantime I will polish up my history and my knowledge of paintings. I would not wish you to catch me out, Vanessa!"

"I am sure I would never be able to do that," she answered in her soft voice, "but I shall try, because it would be a great achievement to do so."

There was, he thought, a mischievous look in her eyes that he had not seen before.

He seemed very tall and large in the small Sitting-Room.

Vanessa had risen too and for a moment they stood facing each other, then the Marquis took the hand she held out to him and raised it to his lips.

"Until tomorrow, Vanessa," he said quietly, and turning went from the room.

Vanessa knew that Dorcas was waiting in the hall to show the Marquis out and she made no attempt to follow him.

Instead she stood in front of the mantelshelf and saw him pass down the little flagged path to the iron gate.

His horses having been walked round the Square,

the phaeton was now waiting outside and she saw him climb into the seat and pick up the reins.

The groom ran to jump up behind and with a flick of the whip the Marquis started his horses.

Vanessa could see his high hat silhouetted against the trees and just for a moment she saw his clear-cut profile and the breadth of his shoulders as he drove away.

"He is magnificent!" she told herself and felt her heart beating unaccountably quickly.

She had never expected to see him again.

How could she have guessed that he would trouble to find her father's address from the Prince of Wales and call with the excuse that he had some miniatures to be restored?

She was quite certain in her own heart that it was not the miniatures which had brought him to Islington but, incredible though it seemed, his wish to see her again.

She thought, when Dorcas had found her to say that the Marquis had arrived, that she must be dreaming. Then she had felt that she could not meet him again and must make some excuse to send him away.

It was impossible for her to explain even to herself how she could have allowed a strange man, someone she had never met before, to kiss her.

Granted, the Marquis had been amazingly kind and had saved her from the odious and terrifying attentions of Sir Julius Stone, but that did not excuse the unaccountable fact that she had neither struggled nor moved away from him but let his lips hold hers.

She did not know why it had been impossible to do anything but stand there, a captive to the strange, inexpressible magic which had risen within her at the touch of his mouth.

Vanessa had never been kissed before and she had wondered what it would be like. She had thought to herself that it would be something soft and gentle and persuasive, but instead she had felt something very different.

It was as if she was being mesmerised and had

lost complete control of her will and indeed of herself.

When the Marquis's lips had touched hers she had felt as if he took her into his keeping and she became his.

She could not explain the sensation that he had evoked; she knew only that it was there and that everything was changed because he had kissed her.

When he left, the door had been closed between them and she had locked it as he had told her to do, and she had sat for a long time on the edge of the small bed, feeling weak and helpless.

She could not even now understand how it had happened. She knew only that when he had looked into her eyes he had drawn her towards him and something strange had passed between them so that she could no longer think clearly.

In fact, it had been impossible to think at all. Everything had just happened involuntarily.

She remembered the way his head had bent towards hers; the touch of his fingers beneath her chin; then his lips holding her, possessing her, until it was impossible to breathe and her heart seemed to rise up into her throat.

Even if he had held her closer still, she thought despairingly, she would have been unable to struggle against him!

It was a superhuman effort on her part, when she learnt he had called, to walk into the small Sitting-Room.

'Perhaps,' she thought, 'he will look different and he will not seem the same here at home.'

But if the Marquis had seemed impressive wearing his robe in the bed-room of the Posting-Inn, he was a thousand times more overwhelming dressed in a grey cut-away whipcord coat over close-fitting champagne-coloured pantaloons, and with shining Hessians which seemed to reflect the very room itself.

His meticulously tied cravat was very white against the squareness of his chin and she thought that his eyes seemed more penetrating than they had been in the candlelit bed-room.

Never had she seen a man as smart or as disturbingly masculine as the Marquis, and he made her feel small and insignificant.

"I am . . . frightened!" she whispered to herself.

Yet it was not the fear she had felt of Sir Julius Stone; it was a fright that was almost a pleasure and certainly exciting in a way she could not explain.

Long after the Marquis had driven away, Vanessa stood staring through the window.

She would see him tomorrow and that was what was important.

She wanted to go driving with him more than she had ever wanted to do anything in her whole life.

She sat down in a chair as she thought of it, planning what she would wear.

Her wardrobe was very limited and she had the feeling that in the Marquis's eyes all her gowns, which she had made herself, would seem cheap and unfashionable.

There was certainly no money with which to buy anything new, and she wondered frantically if it would be possible to retrim the chipstraw bonnet that she had worn for several years.

How could she make it more like those she had seen in Bond Street shops or on the heads of elegant women driving in their carriages in the Parks?

She was thinking despairingly of how little material she had with which to effect such a transformation when she heard a rat-tat at the front door.

She jumped to her feet.

Could the Marquis have returned? she wondered. But when she glanced out the window there was no phaeton outside and it was impossible to see who stood at the door.

She heard Dorcas cross the small hall. There was the sound of voices.

Vanessa could not hear what was said but she had the feeling that Dorcas was trying to send someone away.

Then the door opened.

"Signor Barcéllos, Miss Vanessa," Dorcas said, "wishes to see the Master. He insists that it is a matter of the utmost urgency!"

Chapter Three

Driving back to London, with the phaeton once more engulfed in the unwieldy traffic of the crowded streets, Vanessa thought she had never enjoyed a day more.

The countryside into which the Marquis had driven her had been full of sunshine and flowers and she felt as if everything had a dazzling brightness she had never known before.

It was the third day that the Marquis had taken her driving and, unlike the first two occasions, today they had been more enterprising and had ventured out of the crowded metropolis along narrow, less-frequented roads which for Vanessa were more charming and more fascinating than any shop could ever be.

"Do you really wish to drive into the country?" the Marquis had asked.

"Why should you sound so surprised?" she enquired.

"Because the ladies who have honoured me with their company always wish to show themselves off to their friends and acquaintances, or else to be taken down Bond Street to stare at the delectable frivolities in the windows."

48

Vanessa laughed.

"First of all, I have no friends and acquaintances to envy me even in such a smart phaeton or behind such magnificent horses."

She glanced at the Marquis a little mischievously before she added:

"And as to showing myself off, I cannot help feeling that *your* friends would be very surprised to see that your passenger is someone so unsmart and obviously not of the *Beau-Monde*."

"Once again you are underestimating yourself, Vanessa," the Marquis replied.

"I think really I am being practical," she answered. "You know as well as I do that one should never try to pass off a very inferior picture as a work of Art."

The Marquis smiled cynically. Then he said:

"If I did not know you I should say you were fishing for compliments."

"A connoisseur must always tell the truth," she said severely.

"That is what I have always done where you have been concerned," he answered. "So let me assure you I am very proud to take you anywhere you wish to go. And having said that, shall it be to Rotten Row or to the country?"

"The country!" Vanessa answered without a pause, and he said:

"That is what I also would prefer, but I want to please you."

"Can you imagine it would not please me to drive behind the most splendid horses ever bred," she asked, "and watch the manner in which you handle them?"

The Marquis smiled at the excitement in her voice while she felt as if the sunshine was more dazzling even than it had been before, and the country outside London was even lovelier than she remembered it.

Briar-roses grew in pink and white profusion in the hedges. There was honeysuckle to scent the air and primroses, pale gold, on every mossy bank. The

fields were bright with scarlet poppies, white mari-
golds, and the pale mauve of cuckoo flowers.

When finally the Marquis turned his horses Vanessa had given a deep sigh.

"Must we go back?" she asked. "I feel I could go
on driving forever; driving until we reach the horizon
where it touches the sky."

"And when we get there we shall find another
horizon," the Marquis said. "That is what is so tanta-
lising! One never finds what one seeks; it is always
just ahead."

"Perhaps that is what makes life so entrancing,"
she answered. "If we once reached our goal, if we
once grasped and held what we wanted, then there
would be nothing left to strive for."

"But how satisfactory to realise our dreams," the
Marquis remarked.

"Do you really want so much more than you have
already?" Vanessa enquired.

He considered her question for a moment before
he answered:

"You are speaking of material assets. Surely they
are unimportant?"

"They should be," Vanessa agreed, "but they do
make life simpler. It is difficult always to think fine
thoughts if one is continually worrying how to make
ends meet, whether one can pay the butcher, the
baker, or the candlestick-maker."

There was a note of anxiety in her face which
made the Marquis say:

"Are things very difficult for you at the moment?"

"Papa has been ill for a long time," Vanessa replied. "I was growing worried, but now you have
brought us the miniature from the Prince to restore,
that will at least keep the wolf from the door."

She smiled, but the Marquis realised it was with
an effort.

He told himself that while undoubtedly the
Prince would delay payment for the miniature, he
would personally see that Vanessa's father was fully
recompensed for his work the moment it was completed.

"I do not wish to think of my troubles this afternoon," Vanessa said. "I thought yesterday and the day before were the happiest days I had ever spent and now today is even happier."

"Do you mean that?" the Marquis asked.

"Of course I mean it," she answered. "You have been so kind . . . so unbelievably kind! I keep pinching myself to make quite certain this is not a dream and I shall not wake up to find that it has not happened."

"It is true," the Marquis said, "and I too have been very happy, Vanessa."

There was a note in his voice which made her look away from him, her eyes on the road ahead.

He did not speak for a moment and then he said:

"Someday soon, Vanessa, we must talk about your future. I do not like to think of you struggling alone with an ill father to care for and being worried over anything as sordid as money."

She gave a little laugh.

"It may be sordid, but it is still necessary."

"That is what I want to talk to you about."

She looked at the Marquis in perplexity and he knew that she was so ingenuous that she had not the slightest idea that he was ready to offer her anything she required.

The Marquis realised that Vanessa was very different from all other women he had known and that he must deal with her quite differently.

She had firmly refused, as he had expected, the loan of his horses to ride.

"I want to accept Your Lordship's kind offer," she said when he pressed her, "and I have thought it over very carefully, but I am sure Mama would have said it would be wrong for me to accept so generous an offer from a stranger."

"I am not a stranger, Vanessa," the Marquis contradicted. "Every day we get to know each other a little better, and besides, as I said to you before, who would know? And if they did know, who would care?"

"I should know it was not correct," Vanessa said with just a hint of reproof in her voice.

It was an unanswerable argument and the Marquis said no more.

When they went driving in the phaeton his groom sat behind them in the small seat at the back.

He could not have overheard what was said if they talked quietly, but the mere fact that he was there constituted, the Marquis knew, a kind of chaperonage of which Vanessa was very conscious.

She also behaved in other ways in a manner which made it very difficult for him to say all he wished to.

When he arrived Dorcas always opened the door to him and he waited for Vanessa in the small Sitting-Room.

She was never late, and he was quite sure that she was ready long before the time came for him to collect her. But she kept up the formality of being fetched by her maid to the Sitting-Room.

There was an excitement and a joy in her eyes which even a man much less experienced than the Marquis would have recognised.

But always she curtseyed formally to him in the doorway, while he knew she was longing to run swiftly to his side to ask him eagerly where they were going and what he had planned.

"Will you dine with me one evening?" the Marquis asked now.

Vanessa turned her face towards him.

"Dine with you?" she repeated.

"I want to show you Ruckford House," the Marquis answered. "I have told you about my pictures, Vanessa. It is not the same as seeing them, and I want your opinion of them."

"I should feel shy of expressing what I feel in front of your friends," Vanessa replied. "They would be so much more knowledgeable than I am."

"I was not suggesting that my friends should be present," the Marquis said. "I thought that you and I might dine alone together and then I can show you round the house."

"I would love to do that," Vanessa answered quickly. "At the same time, would it be . . . right for me to come to your house . . . alone and dine with you without a chaperon?"

"I cannot imagine why you want to make so many difficulties," the Marquis said with a touch of irritation in his voice. "You have said that you trust me, Vanessa, and if I am able to take you driving, to all intents and purposes alone, surely there can be nothing wrong in dining with me in my own house surrounded by my servants?"

Vanessa looked away from him.

"I want to come . . . you know that," she said in a low voice. "It is just that there is . . . no-one to tell me . . . what I should or should not do."

"Can you not trust your instincts or—your heart?" the Marquis enquired.

"That is what I wish to do," she answered.

"Then do it!" he insisted. "I cannot ask you to dinner tonight, Vanessa, because I am dining at Carlton House with the Prince of Wales. But tomorrow I shall order a special dinner of all the dishes which I know you will like, and afterwards you shall inspect my possessions."

Vanessa did not speak and the Marquis went on:

"There are a great many things I want to teach you about Art—one of them being the art of good eating. A dinner can be just as much an artistic effort as painting a picture. It is something of which the average Englishman and Englishwoman are blissfully unaware."

"Papa has told me how excellent French cooking can be," Vanessa said.

"He is right," the Marquis replied. "One day when the War is over, Vanessa, you must visit France. Their cuisine is an experience that all women should encounter at some time in their lives."

"I am quite a good cook," Vanessa told him, "but it is dull when you have no-one special to cook for."

"I suppose your father is too ill to eat very much," the Marquis remarked, "and as for Dorcas . . ."

There was a note in his voice that made Vanessa laugh.

"How did you know?" she enquired. "Dorcas is

more persnickety, more difficult than the Prince of
Wales could possibly be."

"All servants are the same," the Marquis remarked. "I have heard my valet's views on the food
that I have enjoyed in other people's houses but
which he has considered beneath contempt!"

"Dorcas does not like beef, she will not touch
cheese, she hates eggs unless they are hard-boiled,
and she is always suspicious in case the fish is not
fresh!" Vanessa related with laughter in her voice.

"I will eat all those things and enjoy them if you
will cook them for me," the Marquis said.

"Then I shall have to give a dinner-party for
you," Vanessa answered, "for I feel your Chef will not
allow me into his kitchen."

"Of that you can be quite certain!" the Marquis
replied. "And the one person I cannot allow you to
upset in my Household is Alfonse."

"A Frenchman?" Vanessa queried. "How can you
be so unpatriotic in war-time as to employ one of
the enemy?"

"Alfonse has been with me and my father before
me for fifteen years," the Marquis answered, "and the
day he leaves my service I shall cross the Channel in
a smuggler's boat to bring back another French
Chef!"

Vanessa laughed delightedly.

She enjoyed listening to the Marquis when he
was serious, but when he was being gay and making
her laugh she found him even more irresistibly attractive than she had before.

Living always with older people like her father
and mother and Dorcas, she thought sometimes that
she had forgotten how to laugh and be gay.

When the Marquis was nonsensical or teased her
it was a delight such as she had never known.

As they drove back towards London she found
herself laughing uncontrollably at many of the things
he said.

Only as they drew nearer to Islington Square did
the Marquis say:

"Do not forget that I shall be collecting you tomorrow evening at half after seven o'clock. I dine at eight, unlike the Prince, who sits down at seven. I shall bring a closed carriage so as not to ruffle your hair, and wear your prettiest gown. I want my house to see you."

"It is not very . . . elaborate," Vanessa said in a low voice.

"Because you are a woman you would not understand if I told you you do not need elaborate gowns. That is the truth, Vanessa, and we both know it is not the frame that matters but the picture inside it."

"Nevertheless," Vanessa answered, "I should like a frame made of diamonds or pearls, or even the beautiful enamels with which the Tudor Miniaturists embellished their paintings."

"One day you shall have them!" the Marquis said softly.

She looked at him in surprise, then thought that he was being prophetic. She only hoped he would be right.

Already she was feeling apprehensive as to how she would appear at Ruckford House in the one evening-gown she owned but had seldom worn.

As they turned into Islington Square, Vanessa felt worried just in case by some unfortunate chance as they drew up outside her house Mr. Barcéllos should arrive at the same time.

She had not mentioned him to the Marquis because she felt it would be difficult to explain why she had accommodated him as he had demanded.

He was certainly no trouble, and yet the mere fact that he was staying in the house made Vanessa feel uncomfortable.

She had told herself a hundred times that she should have been firm and turned him away, but she had found it impossible.

She had not liked him and he made her feel uneasy from the moment Dorcas had shown him into the small Sitting-Room.

A man of perhaps thirty-five, with sharp, pointed features and dark eyes, he appeared very foreign in contrast to the Marquis, who had just left. And he looked at her in a manner which she vaguely thought was impertinent.

His clothes were certainly not of English manufacture, and they were also the clothes of a *petit bourgeois* and Vanessa thought that Mr. Barcéllos might in fact be a superior clerk.

He had bowed to her in a somewhat exaggerated way and she curtseyed perfunctorily.

"You are Miss Lens?" he said. "I wish to see your father."

"I am afraid that is impossible, as I think my maid has already told you," Vanessa replied. "My father has been ill, very ill, and the Doctors will not permit him to see visitors."

"I have to see him."

The words were abrupt and spoken with a strong foreign accent that made them seem to Vanessa menacing.

"I have already said," she replied, "that my father cannot be disturbed by anyone, but you can tell me what your business is with him."

For a moment the stranger looked nonplussed, as if this was something he had not expected. Then he said slowly:

"I knew your father some years ago when he was in France before the War. He told me that if ever I came to England he would help me in any way that I requested of him."

"You met my father in France?" Vanessa said. "Yet you are not French, Sir?"

"No, I am Portuguese, as you might have guessed from my name," the stranger replied, "but it was in Paris that I became acquainted with your father."

Vanessa remembered that her father had been in Paris after the Revolution and before the War had broken out between France and England.

He had not been there for long and he had, she remembered now, been collecting some paintings which he had left there for sale among the aristocrats and which fortunately had not been destroyed.

"My father is ill," Vanessa said. "If you will tell me why you wish to see him, I may perhaps be able to help you. My father has few secrets from me."

Mr. Barcéllos was looking at Vanessa in a speculative manner which made her think that he was trying to decide for himself whether he could trust her.

She wondered what possible concern he could have with her father.

As far as she knew, neither her father nor her mother had had any communication with France for years.

"What I require," Mr. Barcéllos said after a long pause, "is accommodation. I wish to stay here for several days."

"Here?" Vanessa ejaculated.

"Yes, here in this house. Your father always told me to come and see him if I visited England. Now I am in England, and as I have nowhere to go, I was relying on your father to let me stay with him as his guest."

"But it is impossible!" Vanessa exclaimed.

"Why?" Mr. Barcéllos asked.

"As I have already told you, my father is ill," Vanessa replied. "There is only my old maid-servant and myself to look after him and to care for the house. It would be quite impossible for us to have a visitor."

"I will be no trouble," Mr. Barcéllos said. "I have business in London and will be out all day. I just want somewhere to sleep."

"There are Hotels," Vanessa suggested.

"Your father is my friend. I cannot believe he would wish you to turn me away from his door. Let me see him. I can explain to him in a few words what I require."

"No, no!" Vanessa exclaimed. "You must not do that, it would upset him."

She paused. Mr. Barcéllos's eyes were on her face.

"Very well then," he said after what seemed a long silence. "You must assist me, Miss Lens. It would not be difficult for you to give me a bed. That is all."

Vanessa had the feeling that somehow he was not only pressing her but also, in some way, menacing her.

She felt afraid, and she had the feeling that if she went on refusing he would not leave the house but insist upon getting his own way.

"The only thing I can suggest," she said a little weakly, "is a room at the top of the house."

She saw the look of triumph in Mr. Barcéllos's dark eyes.

"I thought you would see reason," he said after a moment. "As it happens, your father owes me a great favour in return for what I once did for him, and that is why I know that if you tell him I am here he will beg me to accept his hospitality."

"I am quite certain . . . the room is not really what you . . . require," Vanessa protested feebly with a last effort to prevent herself from being browbeaten.

"What I require is quite simple," Mr. Barcéllos replied. "It is just a bed, together with your promise, Miss Lens, that no-one will know I am here."

Vanessa's eyes widened.

"It is a secret?" she enquired.

"An important secret!" Mr. Barcéllos answered. "You will not speak of me to anyone, do you understand? No-one must know that I am your guest, not your friends, your relations, your acquaintances, your shop-keepers—no-one!"

"There is no reason why anyone should know of it," Vanessa answered.

Mr. Barcéllos had spoken so forcefully that instinctively she had taken a step backwards.

"Before you make up your mind that this is where you wish to be," she said, "I think I must tell you that the room is very small . . . little more than an attic. It was used by my maid, but it is up two flights and she now finds the stairs too much for her. She therefore now has a bed downstairs, and it will be impossible for her to keep your room clean."

"I wish no-one to enter the room, and I shall keep it locked when I am not in it," Mr. Barcéllos said.

"But why?" Vanessa asked involuntarily.

"That is my business!" he answered abruptly. "All I require from you, Miss Lens, is a roof over my head. I will take my meals outside."

That, at least, Vanessa thought, was a relief. At the same time, she felt anxious and uncomfortable.

"Perhaps you had better see the room before you make up your mind?"

"I have already made it up," Mr. Barcéllos replied. "I came here to be your father's guest. In his absence you, as his daughter, have behaved correctly and in a manner I should expect. There is no more to be said. Is the key to the room in the door?"

"Yes . . . I think so," Vanessa said weakly.

"Very well, I will take up my valise," Mr. Barcéllos said. "Then I shall go out. You must give me a key to the front door. It may be very late before I return and I wish no-one to sit up for me."

Vanessa hesitated.

She had an uncomfortable feeling what with Mr. Barcéllos being able to walk in and out of the house as he pleased, it was no longer her own.

She decided that she disliked everything about him: his aggressive manner; the harshness of his voice as he spoke with a foreign accent; the look in his eyes and the manner in which he was dressed.

She wanted to protest; to tell him that she had changed her mind and he could not stay. Yet she felt he would not listen to her and would in fact do exactly as he wished to do.

There was something so forceful about him that she felt as if he swept her aside; as if she were completely inconsequential, no more than a piece of paper before a strong wind.

"There is a key on the hall table!" she said.

He opened the door of the Sitting-Room and turned to give her what she felt somehow was a sardonic bow.

"Thank you, Miss Lens. I assure you I shall be very little trouble in your house. When you inform your father of my arrival, tell him that the debt is paid!"

"What . . . debt?" Vanessa asked nervously.

The mere word summoned up a vision of money.

"Your father will understand," Mr. Barcéllos answered.

Then he had gone from the Sitting-Room and she heard his footsteps going up the narrow staircase which led to the top of the house.

He had left a few minutes later. He could only just have put his valise down in the bed-room. Vanessa was in the kitchen and she heard his footsteps cross the hall and the front door close behind him.

"How could you have agreed, Miss Vanessa, to his staying here?" Dorcas asked. "It's not right and proper with two unprotected women in the house."

"I really seemed to have no choice," Vanessa replied.

"You should've let me deal with him," Dorcas said.

"I doubt if he would have listened to you. Father owed him a debt."

"Money! Always money!" Dorcas exclaimed. "Did he tell you how much it was?"

"I somehow felt it was not that sort of debt," Vanessa answered, "but I may have been wrong. He just intended to stay here, and nothing I could do or say would have had any effect."

"The cheek of it!" Dorcas muttered to herself.

"Do you think I ought to go upstairs to see if the bed is made up?" Vanessa asked.

"It is," Dorcas answered. "I always felt I might get up those stairs again when my rheumatism is better, so I made up the bed with clean sheets to give myself a kind of encouragement to climb the stairs."

"I have told you to do nothing of the sort," Vanessa insisted. "You are quite comfortable in the little room at the back."

"It's all right," Dorcas replied grudgingly, "at the same time, I never feels I'm a-going properly to bed unless I go upstairs."

Vanessa laughed.

"As long as you are comfortable and not in pain, Dorcas, it does not matter where you sleep. I would rather put you up a bed in the Sitting-Room than have you suffer as you did when you had to drag yourself up two flights."

Dorcas did not answer and after a moment Vanessa said:

"If the bed is made up, there is no reason for me to go to his room."

"You keep away from him, Miss Vanessa!" Dorcas said firmly. "If he's uncomfortable—all the better! He'll soon be going back to France or wherever he's come from!"

"I suppose it must be from Portugal," Vanessa said. "He could hardly come from France now that we are at war again."

"He certainly could not!" Dorcas answered. "If he tried to land on these shores he'd be arrested as a spy and shot!"

Vanessa laughed again.

"That is more than likely, considering all the Volunteers who are itching to shoot a Frenchman. I heard the milkman telling you only last week that he would die happy if he could first see a Frenchie lying dead at his feet."

"They all talk like that," Dorcas said scornfully, "but it's my belief that most of them would run a mile if Napoleon did arrive on these shores!"

"They would not!" Vanessa retorted almost angrily. "Do you know, Dorcas, I was reading in the newspapers the other day that for every Briton in the fight against Napoleon, there have been as many as four Frenchmen, Spaniards, Italians, Dutchmen, or Danes. We stood alone against the tyrant and very proud it ought to make us."

"And what's it cost us in men and misery?" Dorcas asked. "No-one's ever better off for a war, as you'll learn, Miss Vanessa, before you gets much older!"

"I do realise it," Vanessa said quietly. "At the same time, I am proud, very proud, to think that while Napoleon has defeated practically the whole continent he has not been able to defeat us."

She smiled a little mistily as she added:

"Thanks to our Navy! And whatever the newspapers may say, I do not believe that Napoleon will ever be able to invade us. There is that lovely rough green Channel between Calais and the cliffs of Dover, and all the flat-bottomed boats the Emperor may build will never get his Army onto the Downs."

"You may be right, Miss Vanessa," Dorcas admitted. "I never did think those foreigners had much stamina to them. They're a creepy, treacherous lot and you've no right to have a foreigner sleeping in this house. We may be murdered in our beds!"

"I do not think we are important enough for him to bother about us," Vanessa said reassuringly.

But however brave she might sound to Dorcas, she felt uncomfortable when she had gone to bed, knowing that Mr. Barcéllos had not yet returned to the house and realising he would pass her bed-room as he went upstairs to the attic.

She had locked her door and told herself not to think about him.

Nevertheless, she had been unable to sleep until finally in the early hours of the morning she had heard his footsteps going very quietly past her door and up the next flight of stairs.

Where had he been? she wondered. Whom had he been seeing?

Then she told herself firmly that it was none of her business. As long as he "kept to himself," as Dorcas might say, as long as he made no demands upon them, the fact that he was in the house need not be disturbing.

* * *

Mr. Barcéllos had left the following morning before Vanessa was dressed.

She heard him coming down the stairs and stiffened as he passed her door.

She listened, thinking that perhaps he would go into the kitchen and speak to Dorcas, who was already preparing breakfast. But she heard the front door shut.

Crossing the room, she looked out her window to see him passing through the little iron gate and out onto the road.

He was wearing the same rather sombre, bourgeois clothing that he had worn on arrival. His hat was a different shape from those worn by Englishmen, and she saw him putting on neat black gloves as he walked away towards the Square.

He looked, as she had thought when she first saw him, like a superior clerk.

"I am sure he is quite harmless," she told herself and thought she was rather foolish to worry about him.

Nevertheless, there was something about him which made her shiver.

She had, however, the feeling that it would be almost impossible to explain to the Marquis how she could have allowed a foreigner, about whom she knew nothing, to sleep in the house.

It was therefore with a sense of relief that Vanessa realised as the Marquis drew his horses to a standstill that there was no sign of Mr. Barcéllos.

"Thank you," she said. "Thank you very much. I have enjoyed every moment of it."

"I have enjoyed it too," the Marquis answered, "and I shall look forward more than I can tell you, Vanessa, to tomorrow night when you will dine with me."

"You are quite certain that I . . . ought to do so?" she asked almost beneath her breath.

"I am quite certain we should both be disappointed if you refuse me," the Marquis answered.

"I will be ready," Vanessa promised.

The groom had got down to assist her from the phaeton but the Marquis remained in the driving seat, his hands holding the reins.

As she reached the ground Vanessa turned to look up at him, her eyes very large in her small face.

"Thank you again," she said. "It was so very kind of you, My Lord."

"Until tomorrow night, Vanessa," the Marquis replied, and, raising his hat, drove away.

Vanessa went into the house to tell Dorcas about her drive in the country.

"I had forgotten how beautiful it is in the spring,"

she said. "Oh, Dorcas, I wish we could live out of London."

"As my old mother used to say," Dorcas replied, "if wishes were horses, beggars could ride! You be thankful, Miss Vanessa, you've got this house over your head."

"We are lucky we do not have to pay rent," Vanessa agreed.

"Scrimped and saved, your father did, for five years to pay off the mortgage on it," Dorcas declared. "And I don't mind telling you, Miss Vanessa, the country, in the sort of cottage we could afford, would be too much for my old legs. At least the tradesmen call here. We haven't got to go traipsing all over the place for anything we want to buy."

"Yes, of course, I realise that," Vanessa agreed. "At the same time, it was so lovely!"

"Wait till it's raining or the pump's frozen stiff!" Dorcas snapped.

Vanessa laughed.

She was used to Dorcas's good, sound common sense, which always brought her back to earth when she had flights of fancy.

"I had best go up to the studio and do some work," she said. "I must finish the two miniatures His Lordship brought me."

"You do that, Miss Vanessa," Dorcas agreed.

There was something in her voice which made Vanessa say quickly:

"Are you in pain?"

"My leg's been extra tiresome today," Dorcas replied. "If there's nothing you want, Miss Vanessa, I think I'll take a little nap. I've cooked a pie ready for dinner and I'll put it in the oven a little later on."

"There is no hurry," Vanessa answered, "it does not matter what time you and I eat, Dorcas. You go to sleep and I will do some of the work I have been shamefully neglecting while I have been out enjoying myself."

She did not wait for Dorcas's reply but ran upstairs to take off the gown in which she had gone driving with the Marquis and put on an old one.

She settled down in her father's studio to restore the miniatures of James I and the Countess of Ruckford.

The desk at which Cornelius Lens worked when he was well was right in the window with, as the Marquis had suspected when he first saw the house, a good north light.

The studio had, in fact, been added to the original building by an Artist, and was actually bigger than was required by a Miniaturist.

Because Vanessa's mother had often sat with her husband when he was working, it was furnished more as a comfortable Sitting-Room than as a conventional studio.

There was a sofa on one side of the fireplace and an arm-chair on the other. There were pictures on the walls which Vanessa could remember ever since she had been a child.

Some of them had been painted by her father; others had belonged to her grandfather.

Unlike most studios, there was a carpet on the floor and only the long Artist's-desk, with its colourful palette and jars full of paint-brushes, was a reminder of work.

Vanessa had already done quite a lot of restoration on the two miniatures.

Now she had only to paint what she thought of as the nicest bits.

This meant bringing out the colour in the eyes and, in the case of the Countess of Ruckford, giving a new lustre to a necklace of large pearls and the big drop-pearl ear-rings falling from her small ears.

Her father had taught Vanessa almost from the age when she could hold a paint-brush how to help him with his miniatures.

He was very particular that every stroke of the brush should have a meaning; that there should be no unnecessary shadows and to take a pride in achieving perfection.

Vanessa had not only studied her father's style of painting, she had also learned from his contemporaries.

Richard Cosway in particular had a method of enlarging the pupils of the eyes which was quite unique.

He used transparent pigments which he discovered could be floated on the ivory, leaving the material itself to suggest the lights in the portrait.

Vanessa had copied this technique until she could reproduce it on miniatures which previously had been badly painted and whose owners exclaimed with delight when they saw them transformed.

Now as she worked on the miniature of the Countess of Ruckford, she used Cosway's method of long parallel strokes often punctuated by numerous dots or small transverse strokes.

She also used the clear Antwerp blue paint of which Cosway was so fond and which he used in many of his portraits.

Vanessa worked until she realised that she could do no more as the light was fading.

Her father had often told her that it was a waste of time to paint unless the light was perfect.

Reluctantly she rose and set down the miniature she held in her hand.

She was sure that the Marquis would be pleased with it, and that was all she wanted.

At the same time, she thought with embarrassment that she would have to ask him to pay for her work.

She and Dorcas were getting extremely short of money and she wished she could spare enough to buy new ribbons for the gown she would wear tomorrow night.

Then she told herself that such an extravagance would be unforgivable. The silver ribbon which encircled the high waist and crossed over the shoulders was quite good enough even though it was certainly not of the best quality.

The Marquis had said that the frame was not important to a picture. At the same time, Vanessa was feminine enough to long for a gown which would look as beautiful as those worn by the ladies of fashion who usually dined with him.

She was aware that his friends were also the friends of the Prince of Wales, and she knew the names of many of the great beauties, such as the Duchess of Devonshire, Lady Jersey, and of course Mrs. Fitzherbert.

"How can he possibly want me to dine with him?" she asked.

Then she told herself that he did want her to do so, she was sure of it.

She felt a sudden urgency to look at her gown to see if there was anything she could do to improve it before tomorrow night.

Leaving the studio, she went up the short flight of stairs which led to her bed-room.

It was only a small room adjacent to her father's. There was a wardrobe against one wall and she opened it to look almost piteously at the small number of gowns it contained.

Her evening-gown, which she had made of white gauze that she had managed to buy cheap in the Pantheon Bazaar, was, she was thankful to note, in fashion.

It had the high waist which had been introduced from France and which was reputed to have been invented by the Empress Josephine.

Vanessa had copied it laboriously from a gown she had seen in a shop in Bond Street.

It was so plain that it was almost Grecian in shape, and because she was so anxious to see how she would look in it, Vanessa slipped off the old dress in which she had been painting and put it on.

She had worn the gown only once, over a year before, but it seemed to her very elegant and attractive.

She looked at herself critically in the mirror.

What would the Marquis think?

She had done her hair in what she thought was the latest fashion to go driving with him. Now she tidied her curls, and taking from the drawer a piece of the silver ribbon which had been left over from the gown, she bound it round her head.

The effect against her red-gold curls was certainly

attractive, but at the same time her eyes were worried. The gown was home-made! There would be no disguising that fact from another woman.

Vanessa was too honest not to admit that on comparing her gown with the elegant Bond Street confection she had copied, it would be impossible to disguise the truth.

At the same time, the Marquis had said that the frame did not matter!

'If only I had some money!' Vanessa thought. 'If only I could buy one gown, just one, in which to dine with him tomorrow night!'

Then she was ashamed of herself.

How could she be so selfish? How could she want to spend so much money on such frivolity when there were so many other needs that were far more important?

She turned from the mirror and lifted her arms to undo her gown at the back. As she did so there came a loud knock at the front door.

Vanessa waited.

If Dorcas had heard it she would come from the kitchen. Then, as there was no sound, Vanessa realised that Dorcas must still be asleep.

There was no point in her being disturbed. She was often awake for long hours at night with the pain in her leg.

Quickly Vanessa ran down the stairs.

As she reached the front door there was another loud rat-tat on the knocker.

She opened the door. Outside stood a boy with a small package in his hand.

"Does a Mr. Barcéllos live 'ere?" he asked, mispronouncing the name in a ludicrous fashion.

"Yes, he does," Vanessa answered.

"Oi've brought 'im what 'e asked for," the boy said. "There's a shillin' to pay."

He put the package into Vanessa's hand.

"I do not think he is in . . ." she began to say.

Then she realised that she did not know if he was or not.

She had been so intent when working in the studio that it would have been quite easy for him to have entered the house and gone upstairs without her hearing him.

"Wait a moment," she said to the boy. "I will find out if he is here."

"Me Master said Oi was ter bring 'im back a shillin'," the boy answered. " 'e don't give no credit ter foreigners."

"I understand," Vanessa said. "Please wait."

She shut the door, leaving the boy outside, and with the package in her hand started to climb the stairs.

She had to lift up the front of her gown to do so because they were so steep, especially when she reached the last flight, which led from the first floor to the attic.

She went slowly up for fear of tearing the fragile gauze, then as she reached the tiny landing out of which Dorcas's old room opened she heard voices.

'So Mr. Barcéllos is in,' she thought, 'and he must have brought someone with him.'

Still moving carefully, Vanessa walked the last two steps to the door and raised her hand to knock.

As she did so she heard Mr. Barcéllos's voice inside the room and realised that he was talking in French.

Vanessa stood still.

"The quicker he's dead the better!" Mr. Barcéllos was saying.

"You mean kill him tonight?" another voice asked, also in French.

"Why not?" Mr. Barcéllos enquired. "I have ascertained the exact place in Pall Mall where the wall is in shadow, and you have exactly eighty seconds from the time the sentry turns away before he turns again."

"And when I am inside the garden, what then?"

"The Prince, I learn from my informant, usually walks in the garden immediately after dinner, in which case you will shoot him!"

"You have a pistol?"

"It is here."

"And if he does not go into the garden?"

"Then you wait until the lights are turned out. The Prince retires early. You enter by the garden door which is unguarded, and for which I can give you a key. I have marked it on this plan."

"Yes—yes—I can see exactly where it is."

"You proceed to the first floor. The Prince's room is the one with the bow-window. There are no guards inside the Palace except for the night-watchmen and you will be able to hear them coming long before they see you."

"I understand—go on!"

"The Prince will sleep heavily. He is usually drunk when he goes to bed. Kill him using the knife!"

"I am an expert at that!"

"That is why we are employing you! Make your getaway as quickly as possible. It is unlikely that he will be discovered before morning."

"You will be waiting for me?"

"In a carriage in Pall Mall. If you use the pistol the sentry will rush to the door in the garden. It will be easy for you to slip over the wall before they can find you."

"If it is later, make a sound like an owl hooting when you are ready, and I will whistle when the sentry turns and the coast is clear."

"Eighty seconds you say? It should be enough."

"It is plenty!"

As if Vanessa suddenly understood what she had been hearing, she turned from the door and, lifting her skirt, went very, very quietly back down the stairway.

She could hardly believe it possible that what she had overheard had actually been said—yet she knew there was no mistake.

Her French was excellent—her mother had seen to that—and she knew that every word that had been said by Mr. Barcéllos and his confederate was inscribed on her mind in letters of fire.

They meant to kill the Prince of Wales!

Mr. Barcéllos was not Portuguese, as he had said, but French! A spy! An assassin! Sent, doubtless by

Napoleon himself, to murder the man whom the French regarded as the real Ruler of Great Britain.

Since the King was mad, the Prince was virtually the reigning Monarch of France's bitterest enemy!

What was more, Vanessa thought to herself, in the confusion and disruption which would follow the Prince's murder, Napoleon might choose that moment for his invasion.

When she reached her bed-room she realised that she was trembling and yet already she knew in her mind what she must do.

Almost automatically, as if her brain had taken control over her fear, she picked up her handbag, which lay on a chair where she had left it after driving with the Marquis, and took out her white satin purse.

From the wardrobe she collected a long, wide scarf which she had made to cover her evening-gown.

Moving very quietly, she went down the stairs and turned not towards the front door but to the room at the back of the house where Dorcas was sleeping.

The old maid-servant's eyes were open but she had not risen from her bed.

"What time is it, Miss Vanessa?" she asked. "I nodded off just when I thought I should be putting the pie in the oven."

"It is all right, Dorcas," Vanessa said gently. "I have to go out for a little while."

"Go out?" Dorcas ejaculated. "Where can you be going?"

"It is important and I will tell you when I return," Vanessa replied. "Do not worry about anything."

"What's all this about, Miss Vanessa?" Dorcas enquired sharply, but already Vanessa had left her, hurrying from the kitchen to the little hall.

She put the package which the boy had brought down on a narrow oak table, then opened the door.

"Mr. Barcéllos is out," she said, "but I will pay you what he owes. It was a key you brought, was it not?"

"That's right, Miss," the boy answered. "A key 'e

wanted made from a wax impression. They're both there."

"Thank you very much," Vanessa said, "and here is the shilling for your Master."

She gave it into his hand, then as he turned to go she said:

"I wonder if you would walk with me into the Square and whistle up a carriage for me?"

"A-course, Miss," he answered, and added with a cheeky grin, "Ye couldn't be a-whistling dressed as ye are in that 'ere finery."

"No, I could not," Vanessa answered. "That is why I am asking you to be so kind as to do it for me."

"Leave it ter me, Miss!" the boy answered.

They set off side by side. When they reached the Square to Vanessa's relief she saw an empty hackney carriage coming slowly round the corner.

The boy put his fingers in his mouth and let out a whistle that made the coachman start.

The hackney carriage drew up beside them and as the boy opened the door Vanessa looked up at the coachman.

"Drive me to Carlton House," she said clearly, and climbed into the carriage with dignity.

"Cor, we ain't 'alf posh," the boy said impertinently as he closed the door behind her.

Chapter Four

Driving towards the centre of London, Vanessa found her immediate sense of shock at what she had overheard subsiding a little.

She still, however, found it hard to credit that Mr. Barcéllos was in fact a spy and that he had come to England to kill the Prince of Wales.

And yet when she thought about it she realised it was in fact the French reply to what had happened.

In February Napoleon, now for over a year Emperor of the French, had been told of a plot to assassinate him.

It had originated in England where, as was well known, the English encouraged and supported a Training-Camp for conspirators and guerrillas at Romsey.

The head of it was Georges Cadoudal, a squat, red-haired Breton peasant of immense strength who was known as "Goliath" to his friends.

He was a hideous man with a bull-neck, a broken nose, red sideburns, and one grey eye bigger than the other.

Unmarried, dedicated body and soul to the Bourbons, Cadoudal had tried four years earlier to blow up Napoleon's carriage, but had failed.

He decided to go himself to France to kill Napoleon and then, in conjunction with certain discontented Generals of the French Army, put Louis XVIII on the throne.

This plot had been communicated to the English Government, which secretly passed details to their agents abroad and provided Cadoudal with letters of exchange valued at one million francs.

Owing, however, to a careless agent, the plot was discovered by Fouché, head of the Police in Paris, and Cadoudal was arrested.

Unfortunately, Louis Antoine, Prince of the House of Bourbon and Duc d'Enghien, was involved.

He was a decent young Officer of thirty-one who lived alone in the German town of Ettelheim, dividing his time between shooting woodcock and attending secret meetings in Strasbourg.

The Duc d'Enghien was a Frenchman and though he happened to be living in Germany he was subject to French law.

Prompted by his advisors, Napoleon decided to act against him, and on the night of March 14 he sent a General across the Rhine with three Brigades of Gendarmerie and three hundred Dragoons, their horses' shoes muffled with cloth wadding.

Silently they ringed the Duc's house at Ettelheim and seized him when he was asleep.

At a Military Court the Duc was charged with conspiracy in time of war. Under questioning he admitted that he had been receiving forty-two hundred guineas a year from England and he was found guilty.

Napoleon showed no mercy. He considered that the Duc's death would be the settlement of a long-standing vendetta, and on the morning of March 21 in the grounds of Vincennes the Duc d'Enghien was shot by a firing squad.

This proved to be one of Napoleon's most controversial actions.

Inside France it was not thought to be of great importance but abroad it produced a storm of anger.

Many foreign countries who had favoured Napoleon or been neutral now turned against him, and to the English it was merely one more action they might have expected from a barbarian.

Cornelius Lens had always been profoundly Royal in his outlook. He loved France and had before the War numbered many Frenchmen amongst his close friends. The Corsican tyrant seemed to him to be out to destroy everything that was beautiful, traditional, and artistic.

For the last five years Vanessa had listened to tirades against Napoleon and it was particularly horrifying to her to know that for two nights she had sheltered in her own home an assassin sent by him to destroy the Prince of Wales.

And yet in a way she could understand Napoleon's desire to hit out at the Prince personally, not only because he was virtually Head of State, but also because he stood for everything that he, Napoleon, could never be.

He might be declared Emperor of the French by a Senatus Consultation, he might hold most of Europe subservient to his Armies and powerless beneath his dictatorial commands.

But he could never possess the Royal blood which ran in the Prince of Wales's veins, nor would he ever be styled as the Prince was—"the first Gentleman in Europe."

For Napoleon it would be both a patriotic and a personal revenge, Vanessa realised, if the Prince of Wales died in his own bed at the hand of a French assailant.

She was so concentrated on thinking of the motives behind Mr. Barcéllos's plot that she did not think of herself until the hackney carriage drew up under the portico of Carlton House.

She looked out to see a golden glow streaming from the windows and linkmen with lanterns waiting to light her way from the carriage to the door.

It was then for the first time that she felt nervous and afraid.

She had realised when she left home that it

would be useless to try to see the Marquis before he left his own house in Berkeley Square.

He had told her that the Prince dined at seven and the clock in her bed-room had told her that it was after six-thirty before she went downstairs.

She was certain that now it must be nearly seven o'clock and she wondered if even the tale she had to tell would excuse her from interrupting His Royal Highness's dinner-party.

She stepped through the doorway and a magnificent Butler in dark blue livery with gold lace asked:

"Are you expected, Madam?"

He held a list in his hand, and Vanessa was sure that all the guests who had been invited by His Royal Highness had been checked in and were already upstairs.

"I wish to speak immediately with the Marquis of Ruckford."

Vanessa's voice sounded less imperious than she intended, and she thought that the Butler's eyes flickered for a moment over her plain white dress and her white neck, which was devoid of jewellery.

"Is the Marquis expecting you, Madam?"

"No," Vanessa replied. "Will you tell His Lordship it is a matter of life and death?"

The Butler made up his mind.

"If you will come this way, Madam," he said, "I will see if it is possible for me to inform His Lordship that you are here."

He led the way across the brilliantly lit Hall and opened the door of what Vanessa guessed was a Waiting-Room for less important people, or perhaps for those who wished to petition His Royal Highness and must therefore await his pleasure.

It was furnished in what seemed to Vanessa to be a luxurious manner, but she was quite sure it was not a room that the Prince ever entered himself.

"May I have your name, Madam?" the Butler asked.

"Will you inform the Marquis that Miss Vanessa Lens would speak with him?" Vanessa replied.

The Butler shut the door and she was alone.

She wondered what she would do if the Marquis refused or was unable to speak to her.

Perhaps he would send an Aide-de-Camp or a minor Official to listen to her story. In which case it might be dismissed as the imaginings of an hysterical woman, and she would have to return to Islington Square.

Vanessa realised how unconventional—in fact unprecedented—it would appear to the Marquis and the other guests of the Prince that she should come here alone in a hackney carriage with nothing to substantiate her fantastic story.

She wished now that she had brought the key with her. Then she knew that to have done so would merely have made Mr. Barcéllos suspicious that something had gone wrong.

He must have been sure in making his plans that the key would arrive in time to use it. There must be a servant somewhere in Carlton House who had provided him with it.

If the assailant with whom Mr. Barcéllos was speaking failed to kill the Prince, well then there was an accomplice in the house, and here again it seemed to Vanessa that her tale seemed too extraordinary to be credible.

Surely in Carlton House, of all places, no servant would be hired without reference; without those who controlled the Household closely scrutinising the man or woman they engaged.

Quite suddenly Vanessa wished that she had not come.

She felt she might be laughed at, in which case the Marquis would be ashamed of her and perhaps wish they had never met.

Even more insidiously the idea came to her mind that he might think she was not only trying to make herself seem important in bringing him such information, but also, worse still, trying to link their names together in front of his friends.

At this idea, which had never occurred to her until now, Vanessa felt she could not stay.

She had seated herself, when she had been left

alone, on the edge of a brocade chair upholstered to match the heavily draped curtains which were pulled over the window.

For the first time since she had entered the room Vanessa caught a glimpse of herself in one of the long, gold-framed mirrors which hung on the walls.

Because she was so agitated she told herself that she looked out of place, and the sooner she crept away as unexpectedly as she had come the better.

She had in fact in a panic risen to her feet, ready to leave the room, when the door opened and the Marquis came in.

He was looking even more magnificent than he had ever looked before.

He was always supremely elegant and impressive, but in his evening-clothes, with the points of his collar high above his chin and his frilled cravat an expanse of spotless white, he seemed somehow different and more overpowering.

There were several diamond-jewelled decorations glittering on his coat and for a moment Vanessa could only stand staring at him, her fingers clasped together, her eyes wide and frightened in her small face.

The door shut behind the Marquis and he advanced towards her.

"They tell me that you have something of importance to say to me, Vanessa," he said. "What has happened?"

His expression seemed quite unperturbed and Vanessa realised with a sense of relief that at least he was not angry with her.

"I did not wish to . . . disturb you, My Lord," she said in a low voice, "but I had to come and tell you what I had . . . overheard."

"What you had overheard?" the Marquis questioned, then added more gently:

"Shall we not sit down?"

"I must not . . . keep you," Vanessa said, "and I may have been mistaken . . . but I heard the men talking in . . . French . . . I listened and it seemed to be . . . something you should be . . . told."

"What men?" the Marquis asked.

"Mr. Barcéllos," Vanessa replied. "He told me he was Portuguese and I believed him, but now I think he is an agent of Napoleon Bonaparte."

"Sit down, Vanessa!" the Marquis said firmly.

He indicated the chair from which she had just risen and seated himself on another, adjacent to it.

"Now, start at the beginning," he said quietly. "Who is Mr. Barcéllos?"

"He came to my house two days ago," Vanessa answered, "and . . . insisted upon staying with us. He said that my father owed him a . . . debt from years ago when they had . . . met in Paris."

"And did you ask your father if that was true?" the Marquis enquired.

"I . . . I was unable to do so," Vanessa replied. "He was not . . . well enough to be . . . troubled."

"So you allowed him to stay in your house?" the Marquis prompted.

Vanessa looked away from him, the colour rising in her cheeks.

She had known he would disapprove and she was sure by the tone of his voice that the idea of it annoyed him.

"Y-yes," she replied.

"You did not tell me. Why not?"

"I . . . I thought you would not . . . understand that I had no . . . alternative."

The Marquis was silent for a moment, then he said:

"So you permitted this man, of whom you knew nothing, to be your guest?"

"He only wished to sleep in the house," Vanessa said. "He was out all day."

"And he told you he was Portuguese?"

"Yes."

"What makes you think he is not what he appeared to be?"

Hesitatingly, her voice low and a little frightened, Vanessa related what had happened; how she had answered the door to the boy who had brought the key and taken it upstairs to the attic, to overhear Mr. Barcéllos talking to someone in French.

Vanessa had a good memory and she related word for word what had been said.

She spoke in French because she felt that the Marquis would then understand that she had not inserted any other meaning into the words than what Mr. Barcéllos intended.

She told the Marquis how she had picked up her purse in her bed-room and glancing at the clock had realised that he would already have left for Carlton House by the time she could reach Berkeley Square.

"That was ... why I came ... here," she finished.

She raised her eyes to his face pleadingly, as if she begged him to understand that she did not wish to intrude, that she had only done what she thought was right.

"That was very sensible, Vanessa," he said. "And now I want you to come with me and tell your story again to the Prince."

"No! No!" she protested. "I could not do that! Now that you know what has happened, you can take the necessary steps to protect His Royal Highness."

"I feel the story would be far more convincing if you told the Prince of Wales exactly what you overheard," the Marquis insisted.

Vanessa rose to her feet.

"If you will ... excuse me ... My Lord," she said in a frightened little voice, "I would rather go ... home."

"I will look after you, Vanessa," the Marquis replied, "and do not be afraid of His Royal Highness. He has every reason to be very grateful to you."

The Marquis had also risen. Vanessa still looked up at him with pleading in her eyes.

She wanted to run away; she had no wish to be embroiled with the Prince or any of the other people she knew were waiting upstairs, perhaps by now impatient because their dinner was delayed.

The Marquis smiled at her and offered her his arm.

"I have never before suspected you of cowardice, Vanessa!"

She knew he was teasing her and she answered:

"I cannot . . . meet the Prince! You know I cannot . . . do so! Not like . . . this!"

She had almost forgotten as she spoke that in fact she was wearing evening-dress.

"You look very lovely," the Marquis said.

There was a sincerity in his voice which made the colour once again sweep away the nervous pallor of her cheeks.

Because he was waiting she put her fingers lightly on his arm and he led her from the Waiting-Room, across the Hall, and up the double staircase.

On any other occasion Vanessa would have wanted to look at the pictures; to admire the elaborate cornices and even the beauty of the banisters.

Now she was too nervous to notice anything, and even when the Marquis led her into the Blue Drawing-Room, she did not see the miniatures on either side of the mantelshelf.

"I am going to leave you here for one moment," the Marquis explained. "It is important, Vanessa, as I think you will agree, that the Prince should hear your story alone, except perhaps for General Cornwall, who happens to be dining here this evening and is Commander of the Troops stationed in London. He too must be informed of what is likely to occur later in the evening."

Vanessa did not speak and after a moment the Marquis said:

"It is of the utmost importance that what you have to say to the Prince should not be overheard by any of the servants. There is obviously a traitor inside Carlton House, and he must not be given the chance to escape."

Vanessa realised that the Marquis had reached the same conclusion she had; but she could find no words in which to answer him and only looked at him with frightened eyes, afraid of doing or saying the wrong thing.

As if the Marquis understood, he smiled at her in his most beguiling manner.

"It is all right, Vanessa," he said consolingly. "You have done exactly the right thing, so do not worry yourself about it."

He went from the room as he spoke and Vanessa felt as if her last sense of security went with him.

She could hardly believe that she was here, alone at Carlton House, waiting for the Prince of Wales. Then she told herself it was not really of the least importance what the Prince thought or did not think about her.

The Marquis had approved; the Marquis was pleased that she had come; that was all that mattered.

It seemed to Vanessa a long time, although it was in fact only a few minutes, before the door opened and the Marquis brought into the Blue Drawing-Room first the Prince, resplendent in an evening-coat of blue satin festooned with decorations, and behind him a lean, rather hatchet-faced General also profusely decorated.

The Prince was surprisingly like the figure portrayed by the cartoonists, Vanessa thought. He was extremely fat, and all the tight lacing in the world could not disguise the largeness of his stomach.

His chins rippled into his cravat and his face was red under the creams and powders he used to try to improve his complexion.

But his smile was captivating and the manner in which he held out his hand as Vanessa swept to the floor in a deep curtsey made her realise that the stories of his charm and affability had not been exaggerated.

"My friend, the Marquis of Ruckford, tells me, Miss Lens, that you have something of importance to impart which concerns my safety," the Prince said.

"Yes . . . Sire," Vanessa answered, "but I must first apologise for coming at such an . . . inconvenient time."

"War itself is inconvenient," the Prince replied. "I understand that you have uncovered a dastardly French plot against my life?"

"That is true, Sire."

"Tell me about it! Tell me about it!" the Prince said. "And let us sit down while you do so."

He seated himself on a Louis XIV sofa and the Marquis pushed forward a chair for Vanessa to sit near him.

Once again she told her story, and the Prince and the General listened without comment until she had finished.

Then the Prince remarked violently:

"It is disgraceful! Utterly disgraceful! Did you hear, Cornwall? Why am I not better protected? How is it possible that the French know they can enter my garden without discovery? Come into my house and murder me in my bed?"

"I cannot believe, Sire," the General answered, "that the assailant would not have been seen getting over the wall."

"Do your sentries in fact look behind when they are marching forward?" the Prince demanded angrily.

The General did not reply and the Prince went on:

"Why is there no-one to guard the door into the garden? There are sentries at the front of the house— of that I am well aware—but the other doors should be guarded too."

"It has never been necessary in the past, Sire," the General replied with an apologetic note in his voice.

"An omission which, no thanks to those in control, has not resulted in a tragedy," the Prince said.

He was now redder in the face than he had been before and the Marquis said quietly:

"I suggest, Sire, that the men should not be frightened away. Let us make quite certain they are apprehended. The assailant with the weapons can be caught after he has entered the garden, and this will ensure that Barcéllos, or whatever his real name is, can be arrested while he is waiting in his carriage in the Mall."

"Yes, yes, of course," the Prince agreed.

"That will leave us only to find out who supplied

the wax impression of the garden-door key, and that should be the business of the Comptroller of the Household."

The Marquis paused.

"As Colonel Gardner is not dining with you to-night, Sire, may I suggest that you send a cordial message asking him to attend you after dinner? In this way there will be no alarm engendered amongst the staff and the traitor will make no effort to escape before we learn who he is."

The Marquis knew the task was not an easy one, as there were over forty servants employed at Carlton House.

"Sensible! Very sensible!" the Prince approved.

There was silence, then he asked:

"Is there any point in us delaying dinner any longer?"

"No, Sire, of course not!" the Marquis replied.

"And you, Miss Lens, must of course dine with us," the Prince said, turning to Vanessa. "I have no words at present with which to express my gratitude for your courage in coming here immediately to warn me of this plot against my life, and I am persuaded you should be here when the plot fails and those taking part in it are arrested."

"Thank you, Sire," Vanessa said in a low voice, "but I . . ."

She was about to say that she thought she should return home when General Cornwall said to the Prince:

"As you will understand, Sire, there are many arrangements to be made immediately. So perhaps you will excuse me from being present at dinner?"

"Yes, yes, of course," the Prince agreed, "and Miss Lens can take your place. That will save further delay, as we will not have to rearrange the table."

He rose to his feet and offered his arm to Vanessa.

"Come, my dear young lady, I must present you to my friends."

"Please be careful not to say anything in front of

the servants, Sire," the Marquis admonished. "In this house even the walls have ears!"

"We will be very careful," the Prince said, smiling at Vanessa. "This will be our secret, Miss Lens. Yours and mine for a few hours, at any rate."

"You are quite . . . certain, Sire, it would not be . . . best for me to return to . . . Islington?"

"I am quite certain," the Prince replied, "that I wish to enjoy my dinner immediately and to talk to you, Miss Lens, about miniatures. I am perturbed to hear that your father is not well. He is a great Artist and should be busy executing those exquisite paintings for which he is famous."

The Prince was so genial that it was impossible for Vanessa not to respond.

She was a little dismayed as they entered the Chinese Drawing-Room to find that the dinner-party consisted of thirty people and she was aware that the ladies, resplendent in exquisite gowns and glittering with jewels, looked at her with unconcealed curiosity as she entered the room on the Prince's arm.

Mrs. Fitzherbert, despite the fact that she looked much older than Vanessa expected, was exceedingly gracious, especially when the Prince said to her in an undertone:

"Miss Lens has done me a great service, Ma'am."

Then as the Prince introduced her to his guests one after another, Vanessa suddenly saw Sir Julius Stone!

She had not noticed him until she was presented to the lady standing next to him, and she rose from a curtsey to see his dark-arched, depraved eyes looking at her.

Her heart gave a frightened leap, but she told herself that she had nothing to fear; the Marquis was there and Sir Julius could not harm her.

"Sir Julius Stone," the Prince was saying, "Miss Vanessa Lens."

"We have met before," Sir Julius said with an unpleasant note in his voice.

Vanessa did not answer. She curtseyed perfunctorily but she did not look at him again, and the Prince introduced her to one of his Aides-de-Camp and a politician whose name she did not hear.

"Now let us go in to dinner!" the Prince exclaimed and offered his arm to Mrs. Fitzherbert.

However curious everyone might be as to why the Marquis had taken the Prince from the room before dinner, and why they had returned with Vanessa but without General Cornwall, it was impossible for anyone to ask questions while the long drawn-out meal took place.

The Dining-Room was even more fantastic than Vanessa had expected: walled with silver and the ceiling supported by columns of red and yellow granite, it was like something out of the Arabian Nights.

Course succeeded course on an endless service of gold and silver dishes and long before the dinner was even halfway through Vanessa knew that it would be impossible for her to eat any more.

But she had not expected the conversation to be so general or so interesting.

She had supposed that Royalty ate with great formality, with everyone talking in low voices, first to whoever was seated on their right and then on their left.

The Prince talked down the table, beginning a conversation or breaking in on one as it suited him, and everyone followed his lead.

Arguments were started from one side of the table to the other, and it seemed to Vanessa that she had never known that men could be so witty, so amusing, and at the same time so erudite.

The Prince had a habit of introducing classical quotations, and he was never boring and yet there was no doubt that he stimulated the minds of everyone round him.

It was obvious that tonight he was at his very best, not drinking too much and making an effort, the Marquis thought approvingly, to impress everyone with how much at ease he was, so that later they would be able to say:

"But not for one moment would I have guessed that His Royal Highness had been told his life might be in danger!"

Looking back later on the dinner, Vanessa thought there was no subject on which they had not touched: politics, Greek literature, music, books, and of course paintings kept the conversation flowing.

But the impetus always seemed to come from the Prince of Wales, who, with a twist of phrase or a provocating opinion, managed to evoke a lively response from everyone sitting near him.

It was nearly eleven o'clock before the ladies withdrew.

"I am sorry to hear that your father is ill, Miss Lens," Mrs. Fitzherbert said as they moved into the Chinese Drawing-Room. "You must give him my best wishes for a quick recovery."

"I will do that, Ma'am, and thank you," Vanessa replied.

"The Prince has often talked of asking your father to do a miniature of me," Mrs. Fitzherbert went on, "but somehow the idea has never materialised. When he is better we must certainly consider it again."

"That will indeed be an inducement for my father's recovery," Vanessa said.

"And do you yourself paint, Miss Lens?" Mrs. Fitzherbert enquired.

"I help my father with the restoration of miniatures," Vanessa replied, "and sometimes . . ."

She paused.

Mrs. Fitzherbert had moved her hand and Vanessa could see she was wearing a ring of which she had heard a great deal.

Mrs. Fitzherbert followed the direction of her eyes.

"You are looking at the eye of His Royal Highness, which Richard Cosway painted for me," she smiled.

She drew the ring from her finger as she spoke and handed it to Vanessa.

"I have always wanted to see this," Vanessa said. "It is very beautiful, Ma'am."

"It was a clever idea, was it not?" Mrs. Fitzherbert replied. "I think it must have been in 1785 that Mr. Cosway suggested it to His Royal Highness."

Vanessa was staring at the ring which Mrs. Fitzherbert had handed to her. Set in gold with a small circle of diamonds, it contained, instead of a precious stone in the centre, a miniature of the Prince of Wales's eye.

It was brilliantly painted in Richard Cosway's inimitable manner, and it might, Vanessa thought, have been aptly described in the conventional term as a "speaking likeness."

"He made two rings," Mrs. Fitzherbert said. "The Prince often wears the other one, which depicts my eye, and tonight I thought I would wear mine, which shows his. I have not worn it for a long time."

"You set a fashion, Ma'am," Vanessa smiled. "I have heard my father say that when the story became known about your rings, every Artist was besieged by people wanting the eye of the person they loved."

She smiled and added:

"My father was even asked to paint the eye of a favourite horse!"

Mrs. Fitzherbert laughed.

Vanessa handed her back the ring.

"Thank you for letting me see it, Ma'am," she said. "It is in fact the most beautifully painted eye I have ever seen."

"Mr. Cosway is a genius in his own way," Mrs. Fitzherbert remarked.

But she spoke in a somewhat reproving tone and Vanessa was sure that she disapproved of Cosway's mode of life.

The gentlemen joined the ladies a few minutes later, and the Prince had hardly crossed the room to Mrs. Fitzherbert's side before General Cornwall came into the Drawing-Room.

He bowed to the Prince and said:

"Both the French assassins have been arrested, Sire, and taken to the Tower of London!"

"Assassins? What is this?" Mrs. Fitzherbert ejaculated before anyone could speak.

"Colonel Gardner has also asked me to inform you, Your Royal Highness," the General went on, "that a kitchen-boy recently taken into your service has been arrested as being under suspicion of collaborating with the arrested men."

The Prince let out a sigh which seemed to shake the whole of his large body.

"Then tonight, at any rate, General, we can sleep in peace," he said. "At the same time, I hope you have improved the security of Carlton House."

"I have indeed, Sire," the General replied. "There will be no chance of such a situation arising in the future."

"I should hope not! I should hope not!" the Prince remarked.

"Will someone tell me what all this is about?" Mrs. Fitzherbert questioned.

The Marquis obliged, and the whole company listened spell-bound as he told them briefly what Vanessa had overheard.

As he finished speaking Mrs. Fitzherbert with a suspicion of tears in her voice said:

"Miss Lens, how can we ever be grateful enough to you? If this dastardly plot had succeeded it would have been a blow which struck at the very heart of England. I am sure that the morale of our Troops would have been affected."

"It would indeed," the Marquis answered, "and everyone of us owes Miss Lens an inestimable debt of gratitude."

He looked round at the Prince's guests and added:

"At the same time, I feel sure His Royal Highness would not wish this story to be repeated outside these walls. It would reflect badly on those who are responsible for the safety of the Royal family. It might also encourage other traitors to try to succeed where these men have failed. I may sound over-anxious, but I think that silence is important on this matter."

"You are right! Of course, you are right, Ruckford!" the Prince exclaimed. "At the same time, I would have liked those damned French to know that we are not afraid of them, and that for all their plotting and planning they are exceedingly inept when it comes to carrying out their nefarious schemes!"

"I agree with you, Sire," the Marquis said, "but this time I have a feeling that it would be more effective for them to be wondering what has happened; to be surprised when there is no mention of it in the newspapers."

"Keep them on tenterhooks?" the Prince questioned. "Well, that is not a bad plan! So, as the Marquis suggests, you must all keep your lips sealed. Rather difficult where some of the more prettily curved ones are concerned!"

He glanced as he spoke at Lady Bessborough, who was a well-known gossip.

She made an attractive little grimace as she replied:

"You can trust me, Sire. Your safety is more important to me even than having a good story to relate which no-one else knows."

The Prince, who always enjoyed her spriteliness, smiled, but Mrs. Fitzherbert remarked somewhat acidly:

"I am sure, Sire, you can trust *everyone* here to obey your commands."

"But of course you can!" the Duchess of Devonshire said in her soft, gentle way. "We all promise to be very good, not because Your Royal Highness has ordered us to do so but because we all love you."

There was a general murmur of agreement and the Marquis went over to Vanessa's side and said in a voice that only she could hear:

"Shall I escort you home?"

"I do not want to take you away from your friends," she said. "I shall be quite safe alone."

"Do you really imagine I would permit you that?" he enquired.

The expression in his eyes made her feel a little shy.

"I am worried that Dorcas will be wondering what has happened to me."

"I will ask the Prince's leave to take you away now," the Marquis answered.

As he left her to go to the Prince's side Vanessa looked round for Sir Julius Stone. She was afraid that he might speak to her.

But with a sense of relief she saw that he was deep in conversation with another guest.

The Marquis returned.

"We have permission to leave," he said with a smile.

Again the Prince thanked Vanessa effusively and Mrs. Fitzherbert thanked her too.

"Tell your father that as soon as he is well enough to come to Carlton House I have several important commissions for him," the Prince said as she curtseyed.

Vanessa was glad that she did not have to say good-bye to the rest of the guests, because that would have entailed speaking to Sir Julius. He had fortunately been seated at the other end of the table from her at dinner. But she had been aware that he stared at her.

As she walked down the staircase with the Marquis she was able to look round her and note the magnificent Van Dycks on the walls and the beautiful sculptures in the Hall.

The Marquis's carriage was called to the door and Vanessa stepped into it.

It was beautifully sprung and the cushions were very soft at her back. A footman covered their knees with a light rug and they drove away.

In the light of the candle-lantern Vanessa turned to smile at the Marquis.

"It was not as frightening as I feared it would be."

"There was nothing to frighten you," he answered.

"There was at first," she insisted. "It was not only Carlton House, which is even more amazing than the descriptions I had heard of it, it was also all those grand people, the Prince's friends and yours."

"When you get to know them you will find they are only people like you and me, Vanessa," the Marquis answered. "They eat and sleep, they laugh and cry, they are born and they die."

Vanessa laughed.

"That is a clever argument, but you know perfectly well that they may be like you, but they are certainly not like . . . me!"

"Why not?" the Marquis asked.

"Because we live in worlds apart."

"There are, however, two things which provide a bridge between all worlds, however different they may be," the Marquis said.

"What are they?" Vanessa asked curiously.

"The first is beauty," he replied, "and you are very beautiful, Vanessa, and the second is love!"

There was a note in his voice which made her quiver and because she was so vividly conscious of him sitting beside her and the fact that his shoulder touched hers she looked away.

She stared out the window, although there was little to see except an occasional flare from a linkman's torch or the lights of a passing carriage.

"I am not going to talk to you tonight," the Marquis said after a moment, "but there are many things we have to discuss, Vanessa."

"What sort of . . . things?" she asked.

"Things which concern you," the Marquis replied, "and incidentally myself."

He knew that her eyes widened a little as if in surprise, but she did not turn her head and after a moment he said:

"I think we have been happy together these past days—I know I have."

"They have been wonderful! Absolutely wonderful!" Vanessa said impetuously.

Now she turned to look at him and realised with a little shock that his face was nearer to hers than she had somehow expected.

She looked up at him and her eyes were held by the expression in his.

Despite the candle-lantern they both seemed to be but mysterious shadows inside the carriage, and there was a strange feeling of excitement rising inside Vanessa which she could not quite explain.

She only knew it was difficult to breathe and there seemed to be a constriction in her throat that had never been there before.

Yet there was a warmth and a wonder creeping over her which made her feel as if the curtain were rising on a stage where she and the Marquis stood alone.

"I think it was fate that we should meet," the Marquis said in his deep voice.

"Fate?" Vanessa questioned.

"Fate that you should come to my room that night at the Inn," the Marquis answered. "Fate that I should have felt compelled to see you again. Fate that because we have meant something to each other these last few days, you should have saved the Prince's life."

He paused and then asked:

"Did you for a moment, Vanessa, think of going for help to anyone but me?"

"No, of course not," she answered.

"Have you asked yourself why?" he enquired.

She was still for a moment and then she answered a little incoherently:

"It . . . had to be you . . . and you had said that you were . . . dining with the Prince."

"If I had not been, would you have come to me anyway?"

"Yes."

"That is what I wanted to know," the Marquis said. "I want to feel that whatever happens you would turn to me, Vanessa; that you know I am there to help you and make things easier for you. Do you understand?"

"I . . . I think so," Vanessa answered.

"We both need each other," the Marquis went on, "you need me and I know that I need you."

It was impossible for Vanessa to breathe or move.

She had the feeling that the Marquis was about to put his arms round her and hold her against him. Then as if he changed his mind he took her hand in his and lifted it to his lips.

"We will talk about it tomorrow," he said very quietly.

Then he kissed her hand and she felt his lips warm and insistent against the softness of her skin.

She felt a sudden thrill, almost like a streak of lightning run through her and she knew in that moment that she loved him!

She loved him so much that she felt as if she were already a part of him.

Chapter Five

When the Marquis had left Vanessa in Islington he returned to Carlton House to make certain that the Prince was at ease about the arrangements for his security.

Also, although he would not have admitted it even to himself, he wanted to find out what the Prince and Mrs. Fitzherbert had thought of Vanessa.

The other guests had left, including, the Marquis was glad to note, Sir Julius Stone.

He had realised that it must have been a shock to Vanessa to encounter the man who had frightened her at the Posting-Inn.

At the same time, he hoped that in the excitement of saving the Prince from being assassinated she would not attach too much importance to meeting Sir Julius again.

"The sooner she forgets about him the better!" the Marquis told himself, and was more interested in learning what had happened to the French prisoners.

As he had expected, the Prince had already received a report of their arrival at the Tower and the preliminary interrogation that had taken place.

"I am glad you have returned, Ruckford," the

Prince said as the Marquis appeared in the Chinese Drawing-Room. "General Cornwall tells me that the Governor of the Tower is already convinced that these men acted on the instructions of Napoleon himself!"

"I was afraid, after he discovered that the English were involved with the Duc d'Enghien," the Marquis replied, "that Your Royal Highness might be a target for revenge."

"You expected this?" the Prince exclaimed in astonishment.

"I did not anticipate it to the extent of enquiring as to how closely you were guarded, Sire," the Marquis replied. "I now see it was very remiss of me not to have discussed the matter sooner with General Cornwall."

He paused and smiled as he added:

"You know full well, Sire, how much the Army resents interference from outside its ranks."

"I do indeed," the Prince answered bitterly.

He had on various occasions been involved in arguments and caused deep resentment because of his interest in Military affairs.

"At the same time," he added, "to kill me would be a great coup for the French and we must not belittle the fact."

"As Mrs. Fitzherbert said so truly this evening," the Marquis replied, "your death would not only be a tragedy for the whole country, but it would also be a tremendous blow to the morale of our fighting forces."

Mrs. Fitzherbert smiled at the Marquis as he spoke, and he thought that she was looking tired.

She was of course six years older than the Prince, which made her forty-four, and the fascination of her smile, which had been one of her foremost attractions when she was young, was now spoilt by a set of badly fitting false teeth.

At the same time, since she had returned to the Prince's side after his disastrous marriage had come to an end they had obviously been very happy together. As she had said to Lord Stourton:

"We are extremely poor but as merry as crickets."

The Marquis was prepared to believe that, but

knowing the Prince, he was much more sceptical about Mrs. Fitzherbert's insistence that they were living together as brother and sister.

Lady Anne Lindley had told the Marquis that Mrs. Fitzherbert said confidentially:

"I did not consent to make it up with the Prince to live with him either as his wife or his mistress."

But whatever terms they were on together, there was no doubt that once again Mrs. Fitzherbert was exercising her influence for good over the Heir to the Throne.

Looking at the Prince now surrounded by his treasures, fat but exquisitely attired, the Marquis thought, as he had so often thought before, that the Prince was in many ways a unique person who could not be compared to other men.

He was spoilt, but his taste was impeccable; a man of extraordinary distinction, he drew men of distinction to him.

The Marquis was convinced that before the Prince died he would have given an impetus to the art of living which would continue long after his reign had been forgotten.

The towns his architects were designing; the houses which they built; the gardens and Estates of his friends; all would set a standard which generations later would be admired and copied.

"What are you thinking about?" the Prince asked unexpectedly.

"I was thinking about you, Sire," the Marquis replied.

"And what were your thoughts?" the Prince enquired curiously.

"That you have many enemies and critics, Sire," the Marquis answered, "but they are easily outnumbered and outclassed by your friends and admirers."

The Marquis spoke in all sincerity and the Prince was delighted.

"Thank you, Ruckford, thank you!" he exclaimed. "I have always valued your friendship and you have stood by me in bad times. Let us hope we shall be able to share the good ones together!"

"And may they not be long in coming," the Marquis said fervently, and it sounded almost like a prayer.

The Prince did not care for late hours and after a little more conversation the Marquis left.

He looked in at White's and found himself not inclined to join those gambling for high stakes, and seeing no politicians or Statesmen with whom he wished to converse, he soon drove home to Ruckford House.

His valets were waiting up for him and when he had undressed he dismissed them and sat for a time with the day's newspapers on his knee. But he was not reading.

He was thinking about Vanessa.

The Prince had spoken of her before he left Carlton House.

"A beautiful girl, Ruckford!" he said. "I must give her a present; for undoubtedly she saved my life!"

"I like to think that the assassin would have been apprehended long before he reached your bed-room, Sire," the Marquis remarked.

"But what if His Royal Highness had been shot in the garden?" Mrs. Fitzherbert asked, clasping her hands across her ample breast. "There would have been no defence against that!"

"No, indeed," the Prince agreed. "What shall I give Miss Lens, Ruckford?"

"A jewel—it must be a jewel of some sort!" Mrs. Fitzherbert interposed before the Marquis could speak.

"I will look and see if I have anything suitable," the Prince promised. "If not, you two can undoubtedly advise me as to what I should buy her."

"We will choose it together," Mrs. Fitzherbert said softly, "but it is difficult to express even in jewels what it means for me to have you alive and unharmed."

The two middle-aged people smiled at each other and the Marquis felt for the moment he was *de trop*.

Thinking about them in his bed-room, the Marquis felt that if the Prince had married the right woman he would have settled down and become a family man, just as his father had done.

It was too late now to regret that he had been so ill-advised as to marry Princess Caroline of Brunswick and be forced to endure the humiliations she had brought upon him by her outrageous conduct.

There was no doubt, the Marquis realised, that marriage was a lottery, and the Prince was certainly an example of how a bad marriage could torture and belittle a man even of his stature.

"I shall not marry for many years," he told himself.

*   *   *

The Marquis was thinking of Vanessa when he rose the following morning.

Knowing how nervous and apprehensive she had been at Carlton House, he could not help admiring how well she had behaved.

She had obviously been a little shy, but not to the point where she could not join in the conversation or answer with intelligence those who spoke to her.

Her manners were exemplary, and the grace with which she curtseyed and moved had a sense of poetry about it, so that he found himself watching her almost as if she were a ballerina.

'She is exceptional—quite exceptional!' the Marquis thought.

He had risen early as he always did because he liked to ride in the Park when it was comparatively empty. However late he was the night before, he always exercised himself and his horses before breakfast.

It was a day of sunshine with just a touch of crispness in the air, although it would undoubtedly be much warmer later in the day.

The Marquis galloped his mount until both he and the horse had expended much of their surplus energy, then he turned for home.

There was a large breakfast waiting for him in the smaller Dining-Room at Ruckford House which had been redecorated by Robert Adam and was delightfully Grecian with its apple-green-and-white walls as a background to the statuary depicting gods and goddesses of classical mythology.

The Marquis did full justice to a succulent dish of lamb chops, another of kidneys and mushrooms, and a third of fresh salmon which had been caught in the Thames the previous day.

Unlike his contemporaries, he never drank wine or spirits at breakfast, but preferred the fragrant coffee that was becoming more and more fashionable amongst the *Beau-Monde*.

The Marquis was just finishing his meal when his secretary came into the room.

"Good-morning, Gratton!" the Marquis remarked.

Mr. Roland Gratton was a middle-aged man who had served the Marquis ever since he had come of age, and upon whose shoulders the whole burden of his comfort rested.

"Good-morning, My Lord. I have a number of letters for you to sign and I have placed them on your desk. There is one here, I think of a private nature, and another on which I await your instructions."

As Mr. Gratton spoke he set down at the Marquis's side a letter addressed in a scrawling, feminine hand and from which the fragrance of ambergris rose most perceptibly.

The Marquis looked at it without interest and held out his hand for the opened letter which Mr. Gratton proffered.

It was in fact from the agent at Ruckford Park, asking for instructions concerning some building the Marquis had ordered on his last visit to the country.

He gave full details of what he required to Mr. Gratton and then as his secretary turned to leave the room he said:

"Wait a moment, Gratton."

As he spoke he picked up the letter from the table beside him and opened it.

As he had recognised at a glance, it was from Mariabelle Kerrin.

The Marquis held it some distance from his nose; he had always disliked the smell of ambergris and wondered why all the women of Mariabelle's persuasion appeared to think it was attractive to men.

The Marquis read the letter slowly while his secretary waited.

It was, as he had anticipated, a long and passionate outburst of resentment and pique because he had not called recently to see her.

In writing as she did, Mariabelle Kerrin broke all the unwritten laws that governed the relations between those who accepted a protector and the gentlemen who paid for the privilege.

It was understood that a mistress did not complain except about lack of financial generosity, and that could never be said to be at fault where the Marquis was concerned.

He had in fact been unusually and almost overwhelmingly generous to the attractive actress with whom he had passed an appreciable time of enjoyment up to a month ago.

He had then travelled north to stay with Lord Hargrave, and on his return he had not got in touch with Mariabelle Kerrin either at the theatre or at the house in which he had installed her in Chelsea.

He had of course paid her housekeeping bills, which were quite considerable, and the upkeep of the horses he had given her which pulled the very elegant and expensive carriage he had also bought for her.

She had received jewellery which had been the envy of all her friends, and her dressmaker's bills had certainly exceeded in extravagance any which the Marquis had paid for other charmers in the past.

But Mariabelle Kerrin was not complaining that the Marquis was close-fisted. Indeed, as she wrote, what had hurt her "unbearably" and lacerated her with a "cruelty" that was "indescribable" was the fact that he had, as all the world knew, returned to London and had made no effort to call on her.

The Marquis read the badly written, ill-expressed effusion with an expression of distaste.

'It is always the same,' he thought. 'Sooner or later any woman on whom I bestow my patronage desires not my money, but my heart!'

That was something he was not prepared to give and in fact had never given, neither to the fair Cyprians who should not be concerned with anything so intimate, nor to the many distinguished ladies of his own class with whom also he had spent many agreeable hours.

"Why the devil," he said aloud, speaking more to himself than to his secretary, "must women expect so much?"

"Another lovelorn soul, My Lord?" Mr. Gratton enquired with a faint smile.

He had been with the Marquis so long and been involved in so many *affaires de cœur* that he knew the pattern almost as well as the Marquis himself.

The Marquis threw the letter down on the breakfast-table and, wiping his fingers on a napkin in case some of the fragrance of ambergris should cling to him, he said:

"Pay her off, Gratton. Be generous—very generous. She can leave the house when it is convenient to her, but make it clear that I am no longer interested!"

"A good actress, I have always thought, My Lord," Mr. Gratton remarked laconically.

"Over-emotional on stage, and certainly—off!" the Marquis replied.

He rose from the breakfast-table as he spoke and walked towards the door.

Mr. Gratton retrieved the scented letter from the butter-dish where the Marquis had thrown it, and as his Master was about to leave the Dining-Room he asked:

"Perhaps I should mention, My Lord, that it is Lady Lowry's birthday today. Last year you sent her lilies. I was wondering whether you wished to make the same floral offering this year?"

The Marquis paused.

Lady Lowry had held a very special place in his affections for far longer than most women had been able.

She was very beautiful, very talented, and a musician of exceptionally high quality, dark-haired and with a somewhat haunting loveliness

He had even thought for a very short time that she inspired in him the love he had always sought but never found.

Then, like all the others, he had discovered she was but human clay and had recently become possessive and inclined to complain if his other interests prevented him from meeting her.

"Why can women never understand," the Marquis asked, "that there are other things in life besides love-making?"

He had recently been absorbedly interested in the debates in the House of Lords on the progress of the War and a new Act concerning the abolition of certain social evils which he and his friends believed was long overdue.

His presence was essential on such occasions, and if Lady Lowry had waited for him in vain it was not his fault but the fault of those who had allowed conditions in England to get to such a state that it was obvious something must be done about them.

The Marquis made up his mind.

"No, Gratton," he said firmly. "I shall not be sending Lady Lowry lilies this year!"

The Marquis intended to visit Vanessa in Islington as soon as he had finished with his correspondence and changed out of his riding-clothes.

He had already planned that he would take her driving in the country, but that first of all they would talk together on the subject to which he had referred last night.

Unfortunately, when the Marquis came downstairs, dashingly attired in champagne-coloured pantaloons with the gold tassels on his Hessians swinging as he walked, it was to find one of his brother Peers waiting for him in the Library.

It was only to discuss with him the wording of an Amendment they were to put to the Bill which was to go before the House later in the week, but the exact wording was important.

It was some time before his friend could leave Ruckford House with the draft in his hand.

The Marquis's phaeton had been waiting outside

for nearly three quarters of an hour, the horses being walked round and round the Square where the lilacs, purple and white, were in full bloom.

When the Marquis appeared there was the usual flurry of activity, and even the horses, who had been quite quiet up until then, began to plunge about.

The Marquis climbed into the driving-seat, picked up the reins, the groom released the horses' heads to scramble into the seat behind, and they were off.

The Marquis would not have admitted to pushing his horses a little in his impatience to reach Vanessa, but they covered the distance between Berkeley and Islington Squares in what must have been record time.

When they drew up outside the small building which looked like a doll's-house the Marquis realised there was another phaeton outside it.

It was by no means as elegant as his, nor could the horses which drew it be in any way compared with his own, but he recognised the over-flamboyant crest!

There was an angry look in the Marquis's eyes as he stepped down quickly and reached the front door almost before his groom had had time to get to the horses' heads.

His rat-tat on the knocker was imperious and the door was opened almost instantly by Dorcas.

As the Marquis took off his hat preparatory to entering the house she said agitatedly:

"Oh, I'm glad you've come, M'Lord! That gentleman whom we met at the Posting-Inn is upstairs in the studio with Miss Vanessa. He pushed past me and I couldn't prevent him going to her. I didn't know what to do!"

"I will deal with it," the Marquis said savagely.

Although he had never entered the studio he knew where it must be situated, and he hurried up the narrow staircase to where on a half-landing there were three steps leading to where the studio was built out at the back of the house.

As the Marquis threw open the door he heard Vanessa scream and a second later he saw at a glance what was occurring.

Vanessa was struggling in the arms of Sir Julius Stone.

She was so small that anything she could do was completely ineffectual against his superior strength, and as the Marquis entered the studio Sir Julius was tipping her backwards onto the sofa.

She screamed again as she fell against the cushions.

In two strides the Marquis had crossed the room and seized hold of Sir Julius Stone by the collar of his coat.

He had been so intent on subduing Vanessa to his desires that he had not heard the door open or the Marquis enter.

He was bending over Vanessa when the Marquis jerked him up backwards, and he was in fact off balance when he was floored by a blow to the chin.

He fell, sprawling awkwardly to the floor, and the Marquis stood over him menacingly.

"Get up, you swine!" he said fiercely. "I will teach you to come here thrusting yourself upon a lady who does not want you!"

"How dare you strike me, Ruckford!" Sir Julius Stone exclaimed furiously.

"Get up! I intend to give you a lesson you will not forget in a hurry!" the Marquis said.

Sir Julius was older than the Marquis but he was not a coward.

Slowly, taking his time, because he knew that the Marquis would not hit him until he was on his feet, he rose. Then before he finally straightened himself he lashed out at the Marquis with a punch of his right arm which in any boxing-ring would have been considered a foul.

The Marquis avoided the blow and struck Sir Julius again with an upper-cut which made him stagger back against a table which prevented him from falling.

This time a stream of blood poured from his mouth to run down his chin.

He made no effort to strike the Marquis again but only stood staring at him viciously.

"Stand up!" the Marquis commanded.

"I am not fighting you under such circumstances, Ruckford," Sir Julius said sullenly.

There was a glint in the Marquis's eye as he asked:

"Are you prepared to call me out?"

Just for a moment Sir Julius hesitated. Then he remembered that the Marquis was a nonpareil with a pistol and his swordsmanship was acclaimed by every fencing expert in the country.

"No, damn you!" he said after a moment. "I am not prepared to risk my life for any sordid bit o' muslin!"

There was a snarl in the last words and the Marquis said menacingly:

"Say one more word, Stone, and if you are not out of this room within the next ten seconds I will beat you to a pulp!"

There was no doubt that he meant what he said.

After a second's pause Sir Julius Stone, wiping the blood from his chin, walked towards the door and, picking up his hat from the chair on which he had set it down, left without even glancing in Vanessa's direction.

The Marquis waited until the door had closed behind him, then he turned round.

Vanessa was still half sitting, half lying on the sofa where Sir Julius had tumbled her.

She was very pale and her eyes seemed dark with fear. Then as the Marquis stood looking at her she made an inarticulate little sound and rising ran towards him to hide her face against his shoulder.

He put his arms round her and held her close.

"It is all right, Vanessa," he said quietly. "He has gone."

"I was . . . frightened," Vanessa whispered in a voice so low he could hardly hear her. "I was . . . very . . . frightened!"

There was every reason for her to be afraid, the Marquis thought. There was no doubt in his mind, from what he had seen when he came into the studio, what Sir Julius intended to do.

He could feel Vanessa trembling against him and he knew that she was fighting against her tears.

"Like the Prince," he said gently, "you will have to be protected in the future."

As he spoke he looked round the studio and saw on the table in the window his own miniature and the one that belonged to the Prince.

Their frames were beside them and he knew that Vanessa must have finished restoring them, with or without her father's help.

Then he saw that when Sir Julius interrupted her she must have been working on a very small miniature intended to be enclosed in a ring.

The ring was lying beside it and he saw that the miniature was of an eye only just outlined with the details not yet completed.

It was then, looking down at Vanessa, that the Marquis realised she was wearing a blue cotton smock over her dress such as painters usually wore to keep themselves clean.

Quite suddenly it seemed to him that he had been very obtuse.

"Tell me about your father, Vanessa," he said unexpectedly.

She raised her head from his shoulder and looked up at him. Then, as if she realised that in her fear she had been clinging to him, she moved away.

The Marquis let her go.

"What . . . do you . . . want to . . . know?" she asked after a moment, and he knew she was nervous.

"I want to know," the Marquis said gently, "if your father is really here in the house. I think, Vanessa, he may be dead."

Vanessa did not reply and after a moment the Marquis went on:

"It was foolish of me not to have realised it before! So you have been carrying on his work?"

"There was no other way we could . . . live," Vanessa answered. "The house is mine, but Papa left very little money."

"So you painted miniatures and people thought they were his?" the Marquis said.

"I only did restoration work," Vanessa answered quickly, "with the exception of some rings. Papa taught me how to paint an eye."

The Marquis glanced towards the table in the window.

"How did you deceive people into thinking it was your father's work?" he asked.

"When anyone brought Papa a commission," Vanessa replied, "I told them that as he was ill I would make the preliminary sketches for them."

She hesitated and then she added, the colour rising in her cheeks:

"I am . . . afraid I signed his . . . initials on the . . . back."

The Marquis smiled.

"I can understand why it was necessary, Vanessa," he said, "but now this cannot go on. You yourself must realise that."

"You mean Sir Julius might come . . . back?" she asked in a sudden terror.

"I do not think he would risk the beating he would get from me if he did so," the Marquis answered. "At the same time, there will be other men, Vanessa. You are too beautiful to live alone. Besides, what sort of life is it shut up here alone with only your old maid-servant?"

"We have been quite happy," Vanessa answered. "The only worry has been whether I could make enough money, and Dorcas is too old to go without food."

She smiled a little whimsically as she spoke.

"And you are too young to be without it!" the Marquis finished.

He put out his hand and drew Vanessa towards the sofa.

"Come and sit down. I told you that we had to talk today. This is the moment for us to do so."

Vanessa gave him a worried look and then she undid the blue smock she wore over her dress and, taking it off, laid it on a chair.

She knew that the Marquis was waiting and she sat down on the sofa. He seated himself beside her.

Again he took her hand in his, looking down into it, seeing the sensitiveness and delicacy of her long thin fingers and noting there was a tiny smudge of Antwerp blue on one of them.

She seemed to him to be very childlike, and for some unknown reason, or perhaps because in that moment she seemed so young, he changed what he was about to say.

Instead he rose to his feet.

"I will tell you what we will do, Vanessa," he said. "Hurry and pack what things you need for the next few days. Tell Dorcas to do the same. I am going to drive back to Berkeley Square and order a travelling carriage to come here immediately."

"A travelling carriage!" Vanessa exclaimed.

"We are all of us going to Ruckford Park," he said. "You will not wish to stay here, afraid of who will knock on the door, fearing that your third unwelcome visitor might be worse than the first two."

Vanessa thought of Mr. Barcéllos and Sir Julius and exclaimed:

"Can we really go away? It would be wonderful to see your house in the country! Do you really want Dorcas and me?"

"I want you more than I have time to explain," the Marquis said. "Just do as I say, Vanessa and pack quickly. When I return I do not want you to keep my horses waiting."

"I will not do that," Vanessa said, her eyes shining, "but you are sure . . . sure we will not be a . . . nuisance?"

"I am quite sure of that," the Marquis said, his eyes on her face.

The pallor had gone from her cheeks and the fear from her eyes.

There was an excitement about her now and she looked so happy it was as if she felt she could fly.

"Hurry!" the Marquis commanded imperiously. "We will have luncheon on the way. There is an Inn about five miles outside of London where the food is quite palatable."

"I am too excited to want to eat," Vanessa cried.

As she spoke she ran ahead of the Marquis down the stairs, calling for Dorcas as she went.

"Dorcas! Dorcas! What do you think? His Lordship has asked us to go and stay with him in the country. We shall have to pack very quickly."

The Marquis did not wait to hear what Dorcas's answer might be. He let himself out the front door and drove back to Berkeley Square at the same speed he had achieved on his way to Islington.

Once he arrived, he sent for Mr. Gratton and gave him a whole list of instructions.

The first was to send a groom immediately to Ruckford Park to make preparations for his arrival, the second was for a carriage for Dorcas to be despatched to Islington, and a third to have fresh horses ready to draw his own phaeton.

There was a vast number of other orders for Mr. Gratton: invitations to be refused; engagements to be cancelled. But because the Marquis was precise and efficient, it was in under an hour that he arrived back in Islington.

He found Vanessa waiting for him, wearing a pretty flowered muslin gown she had made herself, and the same bonnet she had worn on previous occasions. She carried a shawl to put over her shoulders in case she should feel chilly while they were driving.

Dorcas was also ready, garbed in plain, conventional black and looking, the Marquis thought, a very respectable lady's-maid who would evoke approval from the members of his staff.

The carriage he had despatched from Berkeley Square was already outside the door. The footmen strapped Vanessa's trunks on behind and Dorcas was helped inside with as much politeness as if she were a Duchess.

"You will be all right?" Vanessa asked anxiously.

"Don't you worry about me, Miss Vanessa," Dorcas replied, "and mind you don't linger too long on the way. I'll be worried about you until I see you again."

"I shall be all right," Vanessa answered with a lilt in her voice.

"And lock the front door," Dorcas admonished. "I

have fastened the bolt on the back and the catches on the windows."

Vanessa had heard Dorcas say all this a dozen times before and she answered with a smile:

"There is nothing to worry about. The house will be quite safe until we return . . . and think how wonderful it will be in the country!"

Again there was that lilting note of excitement in her voice and her eyes were on the Marquis. Dorcas pressed her lips together as the carriage started off and in a few moments was out of sight.

"Now can we go?" the Marquis enquired

"As soon as I have locked the door," Vanessa answered.

She turned the key in the lock, then looked at it a little helplessly. It was too big to go into the little satin bag she carried and with a smile the Marquis took it from her.

"I will look after it," he said, "and if it makes your mind any easier I will send word to my secretary tomorrow with instructions that someone from Ruckford House should keep an eye on the place."

"Oh, would you do that?" Vanessa asked. "It would be very kind. I cannot think that anybody would be particularly interested in such a little house, but Dorcas is always afraid that robbers will rush in and steal all our treasures from us!"

She hesitated and then she said:

"On second thought, I think it would be best if I keep the key. Dorcas would not like to think that anyone could go inside the house except herself."

The Marquis handed the key back to Vanessa.

"It would be a great mistake to worry Dorcas!" Vanessa laughed.

"How well you understand! Since Mama died she has tried so hard to look after me, in fact at times she is quite strict."

"And with reason," the Marquis said.

He helped Vanessa into the phaeton and after they had been driving a little time he asked:

"How long has your father been dead?"

"Over six months," Vanessa answered. "I do not

think he wished to live once Mama had gone. He was always inclined to have bronchitis, and last winter it got very bad, but he would not make any effort to fight against it."

She made a helpless little gesture with her hands.

"I tried to interest him in his painting, in the things we could do together, but he loved Mama so very much."

"I am not surprised," the Marquis said. "I can see from the picture in the Sitting-Room that your mother was very beautiful, and it would be impossible, when a man had once possessed so much beauty, to be content without it."

The way he spoke made Vanessa quiver.

Then she told herself severely that he must never realise how much she loved him, nor the strange feelings it gave her to be sitting next to him.

She had thought when she saw Sir Julius come into the studio that the fear which rose within her was like a deadly poison steeping through her veins.

She had been so terrified when he attacked her, and yet even in the midst of her horror she had thought only of the Marquis.

Inside herself she had prayed for him to save her and like a miracle he had appeared.

It was, as he had said yesterday, fate that he should be at hand to help her when she needed him most! He had saved her again from Sir Julius just as he had saved her that first night when she had gone into his room by mistake and he had kept her safe.

"I love him!" Vanessa told herself in her heart as they left the traffic behind and drove into the open country.

It was like being driven to Paradise to know that she was with him and that he was taking her to his home.

To have been alone with Dorcas tonight in their little house, feeling that they were unprotected and anything might happen during the hours of darkness, would have been more frightening than everything else she had endured in the past week.

It seemed as she thought about it that life had become very complicated.

She had lived so quietly while her father was alive. Now suddenly everything had changed.

The visit to Lord Derwent; the advances of Sir Julius Stone; the way Mr. Barcéllos had forced his way into her house; then Sir Julius again, were a succession of events which made her tremble even to think of them.

But always there had been the Marquis!

She had no need to look at him to know the security of his broad shoulders, the height and strength of his body, the authority in his voice.

With him she was safe and she need not be afraid . . . until she must leave him.

She gave an involuntary little sigh and the Marquis asked:

"What is worrying you?"

"Nothing!" she said quickly. "Nothing when I am with you. It is just that I know I shall be afraid when you are not there."

"Then the answer to that is very obvious."

"What is it?"

"I must be there!" the Marquis said, "if that is what you want."

"Of course I want it!" Vanessa replied.

Then it seemed to her that the sound of the horses' hooves on the roadway and the whirr of the wheels was saying one thing and one thing only:

"I love him! I love him! I love him!"

They stopped for luncheon at an Inn, which was far grander, far more important than that in which Vanessa had stayed the night she met the Marquis.

The Landlord hurried out, bowing obsequiously at the Marquis's appearance and his wife took Vanessa upstairs to a room with oak rafters and bow-windows curtained with chintz, to wash her hands.

Because it was so warm Vanessa took off her bonnet and having tidied her hair went down to the private Parlour.

She found that the Marquis, looking very large and impressive against the dark panelling, had ordered their repast, and was now drinking sherry.

He offered Vanessa a glass of madeira, but she shook her head.

"It makes me sleepy to drink at luncheon-time," she told him, "and I want to be very much awake this afternoon for the moment when I first see your house."

"What have you been told about it?" the Marquis asked.

"Very little," Vanessa replied, "but I feel sure it will be exceedingly beautiful."

"It is considered to be one of the greatest and most impressive private houses in England," the Marquis said. "But I think you will understand, Vanessa, when I say it means much more to me than that."

"It is your home and a part of you."

"I could not have expressed it better myself."

"I want to see all your treasures," she told him as they sat down at the table, "and perhaps there is some restoration I can do to your miniatures. I have brought my paints with me."

"Are you determined to refund me for my hospitality?" the Marquis teased.

"But of course!" Vanessa answered. "Mama always said one should never take without giving in return, and I have taken so much from you."

"There is a great deal you can give me in return," the Marquis said quietly.

"I wish I knew what it was," Vanessa answered, "but whatever it is, you know that I will do anything I can . . . anything that you ask of me."

The Marquis seemed about to say something, then he checked himself.

Instead he talked of other things and Vanessa found herself entranced by his learning and by the way he made every subject seem interesting and exciting.

They did not take long over luncheon: Vanessa sensed that the Marquis was anxious to reach his house and there were another two hours' driving ahead of them.

As it was the sun was brilliant and very warm when finally they turned through two large wrought-iron gates and the branches of the great elms sheltered them until suddenly the avenue of trees ended and in front of them in a valley Vanessa saw Ruckford Park.

She had expected it to be unique, but she had not thought, seeing how grand it must be, that it would have a fairy-like quality about it which made it appear like a house out of a dream.

The turrets of the towers, the cupolas on the roof, made it a fairy-tale Palace, and while the windows glittered like diamonds, the great lake in front of it shimmered like silver.

The Marquis had drawn in his horses and now with his eyes on Vanessa's face he asked:

"Tell me what you think of it."

"It is lovely! And a perfect frame for you!"

He smiled, remembering their conversation, and said:

"Where I am concerned the frame is important. I need one to support me, but you are complete in yourself."

"I wish that were true," Vanessa answered, "but this is just where you should live. It is you . . . every bit of it . . . and I love the swans on the lake!"

The Marquis laughed.

"All women are more impressed by the swans than by anything else," he answered, "but I hope you will also enjoy the treasures inside my house, which, although I say it myself, are the envy of all other collectors, even the Prince!"

"You know I want to see them," Vanessa said softly.

"And I want to show them to you."

He drove on towards the house.

As they drew nearer it seemed enormous, and yet strangely enough Vanessa did not feel that it was overwhelming.

There was something warm and welcoming about

Ruckford Park; something which made her say to herself:

"Like its owner, it gives me a sense of security and of safety! Because I love him . . . I also love his home!"

Chapter Six

"It is so beautiful!" Vanessa said, looking out the window in her bed-room.

The lake was golden in the glory of the setting sun, the swans like galleons were sailing proudly across it, and the golden kingcups were a blaze of colour against the green of the surrounding reeds.

"It's a very fine place, Miss Vanessa," Dorcas replied, "but you shouldn't be staying here alone, and well you know it!"

"Alone?" Vanessa queried with a smile. "There are at least fifty people in the house, Dorcas, including His Lordship's Librarian and numerous other persons of importance I have yet to meet."

"You know what I mean, Miss Vanessa," Dorcas said reprovingly. "There's no chaperon, as your mother would have expected."

Vanessa moved from the window to the dressing-table to look at her reflection in the mirror.

"I can quite understand that would be necessary if the Marquis were like other men," she said in a low voice. "But he is different, Dorcas, very different!"

As she spoke she was thinking of Sir Julius Stone, and for a moment there was in her eyes an echo of the fear that he had evoked in her. Then she remembered that there was no reason for her ever to be frightened again.

Never had she imagined that anything could be so beautiful as Ruckford Park and yet not in the least awe-inspiring.

The rooms were large and, as the Marquis had promised her, filled with treasures, but they had an atmosphere about them which was very different from what she had found in other people's houses or at Carlton House.

To begin with, every room seemed redolent with the fragrance of flowers: there were great masses of them on the tables, banked in the fireplaces which were not being used, and even on the Marquis's desk where he habitually wrote.

"My mother loved flowers," he explained to Vanessa, "and she chose a place for them in every room. Since her death the gardeners have carried on her schemes, arranging flowers just as she would have liked them at every season of the year."

The Marquis had shown Vanessa round some of the more important State-Rooms on the afternoon of her arrival, but there had been no time to see a great deal before they must change for dinner.

Today he had continued his tour, telling Vanessa stories about everything he had collected while she listened to him like a child, enthralled with everything he said.

She had, to her delight, found some miniatures which definitely needed restoration.

"Now I can do something for you," Vanessa said.

She thought there was a strange expression on his face and added a little anxiously:

"That is, if you will entrust them to me? I realise they are very valuable and you might therefore prefer to employ an Artist with more experience."

"I am prepared to entrust everything I possess to you, Vanessa," the Marquis answered.

She had smiled at him gratefully and gone on to talk about the miniatures, exclaiming with pleasure when she found how old some of them were, and find-

ing a likeness to the Marquis in his ancestors who
had been painted by Hans Holbein and Nicholas Hilliard.

There was so much to see, so much to talk about,
that Vanessa found the hours slipped by with an en-
chantment she had never known.

The Marquis had taken her riding first thing in
the morning. She had been shy and a little nervous,
not only that he might not think her proficient enough
to ride his thoroughbred animals, but also because he
might be ashamed of her appearance.

Her riding-habit was very old, in fact she had
worn it since she was fifteen. It had been let out her
last years in the country, so there were marks down
the seams, yet even so it was a little too tight.

However, the Marquis had not seemed to notice,
and Vanessa was relieved to find that she had not lost
her touch on the reins, and the Marquis had indeed
complimented her on her seat.

"There are many places on my Estate where we
can ride," he said, "but I am not going to take you too
far this morning for fear you should be tired. You are
likely to be stiff after not having been in the saddle
for so long."

"It does not matter if I am," Vanessa replied. "It
is so wonderful to be riding again and to be with . . .
you."

She looked very lovely in the morning sunshine
as she raised her eyes to his and when he smiled at
her in response she thought that she had never been
so happy.

Then had come their tour of the house and in the
afternoon they had walked in the garden, finding
other beauties in the herb-garden; the old sun-dial
enclosed by Elizabethan brick walls; the velvet green
lawns which led to a Grecian Temple or piece of
Italian statuary which had been brought to Ruckford
House by one of the Marquis's ancestors.

"I have so much to learn," Vanessa said with a little sigh as they returned to the house.

"With someone who is very eager to teach you!"
the Marquis answered.

"You will not find it boring?" Vanessa asked a little anxiously.

"I have never before found anything quite so absorbingly interesting," the Marquis replied.

When Vanessa went upstairs to change for dinner she had thought as she looked at the portraits of the Marquis's ancestors hanging on the walls that they had never ceased to be part of the great house in which they had lived and to which they had contributed so many treasures.

It was almost, she thought whimsically, as if they were still there, moving quietly amongst the passages, content to be still at home and finding that even Paradise faded in comparison to the house they had loved.

Dorcas was waiting to help Vanessa change into her evening-gown. The only "fly in the ointment," as Dorcas herself would have expressed it, was that she had only one evening-dress and she had worn it the night before.

She wondered if the Marquis would notice, but remembered once again that he had said the frame was not important.

Nevertheless, however comforting that thought might be, it gave her a little pang in her heart to know that whilst everything about him was so magnificent, she must appear very simple and unadorned.

"Supposing I had a gown such as Mrs. Fitzherbert was wearing the other night," she asked herself, "with jewels round my neck like the Duchess of Devonshire. Would he admire me more?"

It was a question she was incapable of answering, but she watched Dorcas anxiously as she arranged her hair in a fashion they had tried to copy from *The Ladies Journal* and assisted her to thread the silver ribbon through the curls on the top of her head.

"You look very pretty, Miss Vanessa," Dorcas said, but there was a note in her voice that seemed to be more worried then complimentary.

"I hope His Lordship will think so," Vanessa answered.

She rose, picking up her handkerchief from the dressing-table.

"Good-night, Dorcas. I hope you are enjoying being here in this wonderful house as much as I am."

"I'll wait up for you, Miss Vanessa," Dorcas replied.

"But of course you must do nothing of the kind," Vanessa protested. "Besides, I will be later tonight. Last night I disgraced myself."

"In what way?" Dorcas asked.

"When dinner was over I almost fell asleep," Vanessa replied. "I suppose it must have been the excitement, the fact that I had not slept the night before, and also because . . . Sir Julius had upset me."

Her voice had a perceptible quiver in it at the thought of him, then she continued:

"I was sitting in a chair while His Lordship was talking to me, and quite suddenly I felt my head nodding and my eye-lids dropping. I sat up with a jerk and started to apologise, but he said:

"'Go to bed, Vanessa. As might be expected, you are exhausted, and I should have sent you upstairs as soon as we finished dinner.'

"I wanted to argue," Vanessa went on, "but he would not listen to me. So of course I obeyed him and did as he wished."

She smiled at her maid.

"Tonight I feel as if I have been resting all day, so there will be no need for me to come up to bed until His Lordship also wishes to retire."

"I'll still wait up for you, Miss Vanessa," Dorcas said firmly.

"If you do I shall be very angry," Vanessa replied. "You know you get tired very easily, Dorcas, and you should rest your leg."

She paused and, seeing that the old maid-servant was not convinced, added:

"You would not wish to be ill in a strange house? That would be too embarrassing."

"Well, perhaps I'll tell one of the housemaids to listen for your bell," Dorcas said at length grudgingly.

"You need not waste your breath!" Vanessa answered. "I have always put myself to bed and I am quite capable of doing so now, I can assure you."

"Mind you lock your door, Miss Vanessa."

There was sheer astonishment on Vanessa's face as she turned to look at her maid.

"Lock my door?" she questioned. "Here, at Ruckford Park? Really, Dorcas, you must have robbers and thieves on the brain if you think anyone could disturb us here. Why, there are no less than four night-watchmen in the house—His Lordship told me so himself."

"All the same . . ." Dorcas began.

"I am not going to argue," Vanessa said. "Our troubles and fears are over, Dorcas, we are safe here . . . completely and absolutely safe!"

She bent down as she spoke and kissed Dorcas on the cheek.

"Go to bed and stop fussing," she said. "There is nothing to worry about . . . of that I can assure you!"

She went from the room before Dorcas could speak, eager to hurry downstairs to find the Marquis. She did not see the old woman looking after her with anxious eyes.

The Marquis was waiting for her in the Silver Drawing-Room where the French windows opened out onto a terrace.

He was standing by the mantelshelf as Vanessa entered the room and without in the least intending to she ran towards him.

"As I came down the stairs," she said, "I was trying to think of a way to thank you . . . but I have no . . . words."

He looked down at the happiness in her face.

"You have enjoyed today?"

"It has been utterly and completely wonderful!"

"That is what I have felt too."

He spoke quietly but it seemed to Vanessa as if their words did not even begin to express what was in their thoughts.

The Marquis turned away to fetch her a glass of wine from a silver tray which stood on a side-table.

Vanessa sipped it.

"Champagne?" she asked. "What are we celebrating?"

"Being together!" the Marquis answered. "I think that calls for a very special celebration."

"But of course it does!" Vanessa agreed. "I feel that you have introduced me to another world; a world that I did not even know existed."

"A world you like?" the Marquis enquired.

She gave a little laugh.

"What an inadequate word to describe anything so perfect, so wonderful, and so safe!"

"That is important," the Marquis exclaimed. "I want you to feel safe. You told me that you felt safe when I am with you, and here we are together, Vanessa."

"Together," she repeated.

Somehow it was hard to say the word.

Whatever they ate seemed to be more delicious than the food they had eaten the night before, and yet Vanessa found it difficult to taste the exotic dishes that were presented one after another because she was listening to the Marquis.

They talked of so many things: the house and its history; politics and the Bill the Marquis was intending to support when it came before the House of Lords; painting, pictures, and the Miniaturists who, the Marquis said, looked on life in a different way from other people.

"Why should you think that?" Vanessa asked.

"Because their work is so small that it has to be perfect," he replied. "It is after all perfection that we all seek, Vanessa."

"Is that what you want to find?"

"It is what I have always looked for," he answered, "and now I think I have found it."

She did not understand what he meant, and as she looked at him enquiringly he rose from the table.

"Come," he said, "I am going to bring my port with me into the Drawing-Room so that you need not leave me."

"I certainly do not want to leave you."

"Are you sure about that?"

"Of course. When you are not there, everywhere seems very empty."

She spoke lightly, but there was a look of satisfaction in the Marquis's eyes as he followed her down the broad corridor and across the great Hall to the Drawing-Room.

One of the French windows was open and Vanessa walked towards it. Then after looking outside she stepped out onto the terrace.

It had been a very warm, still day. There was not a breath of wind to ruffle the surface of the lake as it lay beneath them dark and mysterious in the shadows.

Behind the great trees of the Park there was just the last glimmer of gold and crimson as the day sank out of sight before the encroaching night.

Above them, the first evening star glittered against the sable-blue of the sky. Vanessa turned her head to look at it, the line of her small chin and long neck very lovely against the grey stone of the house.

The Marquis leant against the balustrade.

She lowered her eyes towards the lake and saw the evening mist almost like the movement of water-nymphs rising about it.

"It is all so beautiful!" she said in a soft voice. "I feel it must be a dream."

"Just as you are a dream! A dream which for me has come true!"

There was a note in his voice which made her turn to look at him.

"I did not believe that anyone could be so beautiful and so perfect."

"Do you . . . mean that?"

"I mean it."

She looked up at him and was unable to breathe. Then as if she moved unconsciously, without any effort of will, she drew closer and he put his arms round her.

"I have been searching for you, Vanessa, all through my life, and now that I have found you I can never let you go."

He saw the radiance that came into her face, then slowly, as if he would not frighten her, he bent his head and found her lips.

For Vanessa it was a moment of surprise and then of wonder, until as she felt his mouth take possession of hers a rapture such as she had never believed existed swept through her so that she became a part of him.

They were one and at the same time the glory of the sunset, the mystery of the night, and the beauty of the lake was part of them both.

The Marquis drew her still closer and Vanessa felt as if her whole body melted into his.

She knew then that this was love and it was beyond anything she had ever known or imagined.

It was a rapture, an ecstasy, and a beauty surpassing beauty itself, and because it was to her Divine, she felt as if the Marquis carried her up into the sky.

'This is the love of God,' she thought as she felt that his kiss drew her soul from between her lips and she no longer belonged to herself.

Only as the Marquis raised his head to look down at her did she realise that she was trembling.

"I . . . love . . . you!" she whispered.

"Oh, my precious, my darling!" the Marquis exclaimed. "That is what I wanted you to tell me."

"I love . . . you!" she repeated, as if the words must express some of the wonder within herself.

He kissed her again until she felt as if her feet were no longer on the ground and the world spun round them and no longer existed.

"I love . . . you! I . . . love you!"

She was not sure whether she was saying the words or whether they were merely a part of the throbbing in her heart, while the thrills which ran through her made her feel as if he had brought her to life and she had never lived before.

How long they stood on the terrace was impossible to know. Only at last the Marquis drew Vanessa back through the open window and into the Drawing-Room.

"You must not get cold," he said gently, "and anyway I want to talk to you, my darling."

"Have we really anything to say to each other?" Vanessa asked.

He looked down at the glory in her eyes and smiled.

"Nothing of any importance, my lovely one. You told me all I wished to hear when you said you loved me."

"I did not know it myself at first," she whispered, "and then I knew I must have . . . loved you from the moment you first kissed me."

"I could not prevent myself. Then when I touched your lips, Vanessa, I knew that fate had brought you into my life and there would be no escape for either of us."

"You would not . . . wish to escape?"

He laughed at the sudden anxiety in her voice and kissed her again before they sat down on the sofa and she laid her head confidingly against his shoulder.

"I did not believe such happiness existed," the Marquis said, and she knew that he spoke the truth.

"It is like a dream . . . that I should love you and that everything about you should be so . . . splendid; so utterly . . . wonderful!"

There was so much awe in her voice that the Marquis's arm tightened about her as he said:

"You must not expect too much of me, Vanessa. I am only a man, and as such very fallible."

"But a wonderful man!" Vanessa said softly. "How can I have found someone like . . . you?"

"And yet you hoped to find me, even as I hoped to find you?" the Marquis asked.

"I think that ever since I began painting I have wanted to paint your face," she answered. "It was always there somewhere in my heart. Perhaps in a special shrine where I worshipped without realising exactly what I was doing."

"My precious, how can you say such things to me?" the Marquis asked and kissed her again.

Because the passion and possessiveness of his kisses aroused new sensations within her, Vanessa hid her face against him and the Marquis looked down at her with a very tender smile on his lips.

"Do I excite you a little, Vanessa?"

"You give me very . . . strange . . . feelings. It is not only my heart that . . . responds to you . . . but also my whole body . . . which seems to vibrate to a magic tune. It is wonderful . . . thrilling, and perhaps also a little . . . frightening."

"I would never frighten you, my darling. But you belong to me and now we must make plans for the future."

Vanessa's face was still hidden against his shoulder and he kissed her hair before he said:

"I will buy a house as near to Berkeley Square as possible, perhaps in Charles Street. I will staff it with servants who will take great care of you and we will spend as much time as possible together."

As the Marquis finished speaking he felt Vanessa go stiff in his arms, then slowly she raised her head.

"A . . . house?" she questioned.

"You cannot go on living alone in Islington," the Marquis explained, "and I want you as near to me as possible. When the War is over, we will go abroad at least once a year and sometime this summer we will journey to Cornwall, where I have Estates."

The Marquis stopped suddenly.

He realised that Vanessa was looking at him, her eyes wide and questioning, and he ceased putting his plans into words.

"What are you . . . asking me to . . . do?" Vanessa queried, her voice trembling.

The Marquis looked into her eyes, then as she moved a little further away from him he said:

"I thought you understood, Vanessa! This is something I have been trying to say for the last two days. I want to protect you and keep you from everything and everybody who might frighten you in the future."

"But . . . I thought . . ." Vanessa began hardly above a whisper.

The Marquis looked away from her and rose to his feet.

He could not pretend to himself that he did not know what Vanessa had thought or what she had expected.

"This is hard to explain," he said after a moment.

He stood facing the fireplace, but he knew that Vanessa had turned very pale and her eyes seemed unnaturally large in her small face.

"I . . . I thought you . . . loved me."

The words were very low and lost, as if she spoke to herself.

"I have told you, Vanessa, what you mean to me," the Marquis said. "I want you to be with me more than I can possibly express in words."

He drew in his breath, then added firmly:

"But I cannot offer you marriage!"

There was a silence in the Drawing-Room and the tick of the small clock on the mantelshelf seemed very loud.

Vanessa did not speak and after a moment the Marquis went on:

"You know that my family is a very old one and we have always played a part in the history of England. Well, this entails certain obligations upon those who hold the title and occupy the position I have inherited."

The Marquis paused as if he expected Vanessa to speak but no sound came from her lips, and he continued:

"When I marry, which will not be for many years, I have to choose someone whose family equals mine in rank and importance. It is what will be expected of me and is a responsibility I must accept because of the privileges I enjoy. I want you to understand this, Vanessa and know that it does not in any way affect my feelings for you."

The Marquis waited and after a moment Vanessa said hesitatingly:

"What . . . you are . . . asking is that I should . . . live with you until you . . . tire of me?"

The Marquis turned to face her.

"It would not be like that, Vanessa, that I promise you. I know as surely as I know that I am alive that we shall never tire of each other. We will be together and there is all the happiness in the world waiting for us in the future."

There was, however, no happiness in Vanessa's face.

The radiance that had transformed her had vanished, and her eyes as she looked at him seemed full of shadow and he could not read the expression in them.

"Trust me," the Marquis said insistently. "Trust me, Vanessa! I swear that I will look after you from this moment until I die! You will be rich! There will be nothing you require which I cannot give you!"

For the first time since he had begun to speak, Vanessa moved and made an impatient little gesture with her hand as if she swept away all that he offered her.

Then she said in a very low, hesitating voice:

"When Sir Julius Stone was in the . . . studio yesterday he . . . referred to me in a . . . certain way which made you . . . angry. But if I . . . do as you suggest . . . that is . . . exactly what I . . . should . . . be."

"Stone is a foul-mouthed swine!" the Marquis said angrily. "You would never be anything but the woman I honour and respect as part of myself."

There was silence and after a moment he went on:

"Think what will be the alternative, Vanessa. If you will not stay with me, what future will you have without money, without protection? Do you really imagine that you and Dorcas can continue to battle on alone? Remember, there will always be men like Julius Stone in the world."

He saw Vanessa give a little quiver of fear and relentlessly, because he was intent upon getting his own way, he continued:

"Living as you have been doing, Vanessa, is inviting trouble and even disaster, if I am not there to protect you."

The Marquis sat down beside Vanessa on the sofa.

"Be sensible, my darling."

"But it would be . . . wrong!"

"Wrong? What is wrong and what is right?" the Marquis enquired. "Is it wrong to seek happiness, and right to leave yourself open to be pursued and insulted by men who will disgust you?"

He reached out his hand to take hers and found that her fingers were very cold. They quivered in his like a bird when it has been caught in a snare and cannot escape.

"There are so many things in the world that will frighten you, Vanessa," he said. "I want you to enjoy the happiness that I believe only I can give you. You have said that you love me. If that is so, can you contemplate life without me?"

Vanessa gave a little cry and turned towards him. Once again he put his arms round her.

"Try to be sensible about this, my darling."

"Can I . . . can I think . . . about it?"

"Of course," the Marquis answered. "I can understand I must give you time to get used to the idea. When you come to think it over I know you will realise that it is the only solution to your problems and —mine."

He felt, although she did not speak, that she questioned what his difficulty could be and he added:

"My problem is quite simple, Vanessa: I cannot live without you!"

He felt her tremble against him and holding her closer he said:

"There is so much I want to teach you; so much we can do together; so much we can discover about each other. Oh, my dearest, do not keep me waiting too long."

There was a sudden note of passion in the Marquis's voice and then as Vanessa did not answer he put his fingers under her chin and turned her face up to his.

"I want you!" he said in his deep voice. "God knows I want you as I have never wanted a woman before in the whole of my life! But I will wait, my darling, until you tell me you are ready to be mine."

He kissed her but somehow he felt as if the almost

unearthly wonder of the kisses they had known on the terrace and when they first came into the Drawing-Room was overshadowed.

He knew that Vanessa had withdrawn a little and she was no longer as close to him in spirit as she had been before.

"You cannot refuse me," he said masterfully. "I am speaking the truth, Vanessa, when I tell you that I cannot live without you. You must give me your love, for it fills my whole world."

She looked at him for a moment with an enigmatic expression in her eyes that he had never seen before. Then with a gesture she turned away from his enfolding arms.

"I want to . . . think. Please . . . let me . . . think."

"Am I stopping you from doing that?"

"I cannot . . . think . . . when you . . . touch me."

There was the light of triumph in the Marquis's eyes as he took his arms away from her and said:

"I set you free, Vanessa, but I am convinced that it is impossible for either of us to be really free of each other."

He thought she would turn to him again, but instead she rose to her feet.

"I would . . . like to go to . . . bed. I will think over what you have . . . suggested and perhaps tomorrow I shall be able to . . . give you an . . . answer."

"The only answer I will accept," the Marquis said insistently, "is that you agree. Please, my darling, do not destroy our happiness. If you love me you will know how precious it is and, once lost, we may **never** find it again."

"You will think it . . . foolish of me," Vanessa replied, "but I cannot decide anything so . . . important when I . . . hear your voice and when I see your . . . face."

"You say that because you love me," the Marquis said.

"Yes, I . . . love you," Vanessa answered, and there was a little sob on the words.

She was standing very straight and still, while the Marquis was still sitting on the sofa, looking at her.

There was something very valiant, he thought, about the slimness of her figure, her small, classical features, and the worried darkness of her eyes.

The glow of the candles picked out the fiery lights in her hair and they glinted so enticingly that the Marquis was sure that once she was awakened to love she would know the fires of desire.

"How can you hesitate, Vanessa?" he asked suddenly as if the words were forced from his lips. "How can you fail to understand that what we feel for each other is different from what either of us could feel for anyone else? How can man-made laws, the restrictions and commandments of Priests, affect what we know is the essence of life itself?"

"I . . . know it is . . . different," Vanessa said, "and I . . . know that I . . . love you . . . but . . . please . . . now I must . . . go."

For one moment her eyes were raised to the Marquis's face and he saw that she wanted to be in his arms. Then with what was a superhuman effort she turned and ran from the room.

He heard her footsteps cross the Hall and knew she would be running up the stairs.

He walked across the room and out onto the terrace.

"We belong to each other!" he said to the stars which were now beginning to fill the sky above. "When she thinks it over she will be as sure of it as I am."

*   *   *

Vanessa slept very little that night.

It seemed to her that two people stood one on either side of her bed and she argued with first one and then the other, until her whole mind became chaotic and she could make no sense of her thoughts.

On the one hand, she knew that she loved the Marquis and that in a way all he had suggested made sense. But on the other hand there was her mother, who had taught her ever since she was a child that love was sacred.

"When a woman loves, dearest," she had said in her gentle voice, "she gives herself to a man for life;

to look after him; to care for him in sickness and in health."

She paused and added:

"She becomes an indivisible part of him and he of her."

Vanessa was aware that her mother had been speaking of marriage, while the Marquis was not prepared to offer her marriage.

"How could I look after him?" Vanessa asked herself. "How could we be one if he only spends some of his time with me? While to the world outside I will be as Sir Julius Stone described me—'a soiled bit o' muslin.'"

Vanessa remembered how shocked her mother had been by the behaviour of the Prince of Wales and Richard Cosway.

When her father had talked of them she would often say when Vanessa was there:

"Not in front of the child, Cornelius. Besides, I do not wish the behaviour of people who should know better to spoil the atmosphere in this house. Talk of them elsewhere, but not here."

It was impossible for Vanessa not to be aware of what her mother would think of her behaviour if she accepted the Marquis's proposition and became his mistress.

Ever since she had been a child people had talked in her presence, despite all her mother could do to prevent it, of the raffish, often outrageous behaviour of the Prince of Wales and the Bucks and Dandies who surrounded him.

She had heard her mother's friends exclaim with horror at the *affaires de coeur* flaunted by the great ladies of the *Beau-Monde*.

And when they thought she was not listening, her father's artistic friends had made jokes about the places in various parts of London which catered for the more erotic tastes of the gentlemen of St. James's.

It was only a word here and an innuendo there, but Vanessa had sharp ears and an even quicker intelligence.

When she had grown older she had realised that

at night there were painted, gaudily dressed women walking the streets, trying to attract the attention of men who were unaccompanied by ladies.

She had even on occasions seen girls who were little more than pathetic children with their lips reddened and their faces powdered.

As she did not often go out at night except to a concert and very occasionally to a play with her father and mother, she had not at first understood the significance of what she had seen.

But now in her mind's eye she could visualise fully the scenes and for the first time she realised the truth.

The Marquis had said their relationship would be different, but Vanessa knew that if she allowed him to give her a house; if she accepted presents, of clothes and jewels and horses, she would be behaving in the same manner, if on a higher scale, as the painted women who walked the darkened streets.

Every instinct in her body shrank away from the idea, even while with an agony that was inexpressible she told herself that if she refused the Marquis she would never see him again.

"I love him . . . please, God, I love . . . him," she prayed. "What am I to . . . do?"

     *   *   *

There were lines under Vanessa's eyes and she looked tired when Dorcas called her in the morning.

"It's a lovely day, Miss Vanessa," the old maid said in an unexpected good humour as she pulled back the curtains.

"Can you find out, Dorcas, whether His Lordship expects me to go riding with him?" Vanessa asked.

"I've a message from His Lordship," Dorcas answered. "He would like you to ride with him, Miss Vanessa, but this afternoon. There's a fire at one of the outlying farms on the Estate and His Lordship was fetched almost before he'd finished his breakfast."

"A fire?" Vanessa asked.

"It started in one of the outbuildings, the Butler was telling me," Dorcas related, "but it has now spread to the house itself and His Lordship has a lot of valuable live-stock on that farm."

"How terrible!" Vanessa exclaimed. "I can quite understand His Lordship wishing to see what can be done."

"If you're going to get up, Miss Vanessa," Dorcas said, "you can put on one of your cool muslins. It's going to be a hot day and you can change into your riding-habit after luncheon."

"Yes, I will do that," Vanessa agreed.

She would have dressed slowly because she was tired, but Dorcas was talking so much that she wanted to be alone and she therefore hurried.

It was not yet nine o'clock when she came downstairs and she knew that the morning would seem long without the Marquis. At the same time, she half dreaded seeing him.

She had not yet made up her mind. She had no answer to his proposition and she wondered apprehensively if he would be angry or irritated because she was being so slow.

She was, however, determined to utilise the hours she would spend until he returned in doing something useful.

She carried her paints downstairs with her and went to the Rose Drawing-Room at the far end of the house which overlooked the rose-garden.

It was here that the Marquis's miniatures were assembled. A number of them were arranged on either side of the Adam mantelpiece; others, in gold cabinets, were displayed on ivory-coloured velvet.

The miniatures by Nicholas Hilliard, Vanessa noticed, despite their unique jewel-like quality, seemed thin and toneless compared with the genius of Hans Holbein.

She was too nervous to touch the Master's work, which was just as brilliant in colour as it had been in the reign of Henry VIII.

Instead she lifted down one which she had noticed was faded and which had been painted by John Hoskins, the uncle and Master of Samuel Cooper, in the Seventeenth Century.

'I will start with this one,' she thought, and arranged her paints on the small mahogany table which she pushed in front of one of the windows.

There was not a great deal to do to the portrait, but she knew the Marquis wanted all his possessions to be perfect.

She had unfortunately not brought her smock with her from London. It had been forgotten when she had thrown it down in the studio after the Marquis had rescued her from Sir Julius Stone.

Instead she spread a linen towel over her gown, and taking the miniature from its frame she very carefully matched the paints on her palette.

She had been working for nearly an hour when the door opened behind her and she turned her head eagerly, hoping that after all the Marquis had got back more quickly than he had expected.

To her surprise, however, a lady stood there, elderly and very distinguished, dressed expensively but not particularly in the latest fashion.

Vanessa rose to her feet as the newcomer advanced into the room.

"You are Miss Vanessa Lens?" the lady asked in a cold, well-bred voice which seemed somehow to chill the atmosphere.

"Yes, Ma'am."

"I was informed that you were staying here," the lady said, "so I called to see the Marquis of Ruckford and ascertain if it was in fact the truth."

Vanessa looked surprised and the lady went on:

"I am the Duchess of Tealby. My son, the Marquis of Gramly, was present at Carlton House the other night when you were a guest of His Royal Highness, the Prince of Wales."

"Yes, Ma'am."

Vanessa was wondering what this was all about, remembering that the Marquis had cautioned everyone who was present that night not to mention what had occurred.

"I understand that you arrived alone and asked for the Marquis," the Duchess continued, "who took

His Royal Highness from the Drawing-Room to meet you. That is so?"

"Yes, Ma'am."

"That is what my son told me," the Duchess said, "but what I could not credit was that you were actually staying here at Ruckford Park."

Vanessa looked at her enquiringly. She could not understand what the Duchess was trying to say.

"You are, I understand, the daughter of a Miniaturist?" the Duchess questioned.

"Yes, Ma'am."

"I see you are working on one now. Is that your usual occupation?"

"Yes, Ma'am. I have assisted my father for some years."

"In which case you have a studio in London?"

"Yes, Ma'am . . . in Islington."

"Then that is where you should be working," the Duchess said firmly.

She looked at Vanessa and her eyes were hard as she went on:

"I will be quite frank with you, Miss Lens. I do not think it at all seemly that you should be staying at Ruckford Park when the Marquis is in residence."

Vanessa gave a little gasp, but she did not speak.

"If you were an ordinary unknown Artist it would not matter," the Duchess said, "but because you have evoked a great deal of gossip in London by appearing at Carlton House and being the guest of His Royal Highness in somewhat mysterious circumstances, people will certainly talk if you are here."

"I am, as you see, Ma'am, restoring one of His Lordship's miniatures," Vanessa said defensively.

"I am aware of that," the Duchess replied. "But as I have already told you, Miss Lens, this restoration work, if it is so urgent, should take place in your own studio."

Vanessa looked away from the Duchess and down at the miniature on the table.

"I feel you are deliberately misunderstanding what I am saying to you," the Duchess said, as if she thought Vanessa was being inattentive. "The Marquis has a very important position in the County and, as you must be aware, it is impossible for anything to take place in a country neighbourhood without it becoming generally known and discussed. The Marquis, like his father, is greatly respected and it will do him considerable harm for you to remain at Ruckford Park unchaperoned."

"Harm?" Vanessa questioned.

"But of course," the Duchess said. "Gentlemen, although you may not know it, Miss Lens, do not bring unattached and unattended ladies into their homes. What they do in London is their own business, but to give rise to a scandal in the house where his mother lived and died will react most adversely upon the Marquis."

"I can . . . understand . . . that," Vanessa said after a moment in a low voice.

"Then I hope you will take my advice and leave here as soon as possible," the Duchess said. "I intended to say this to the Marquis himself, but as he is out perhaps it is better that I have spoken to you direct. I am sure you will lose nothing financially by working, as I suggested, in your studio rather than at Ruckford Park."

She paused to add sharply:

"I am sure too that the Marquis in bringing you here was merely being thoughtless or underestimating his own importance. He undoubtedly meant no harm, but if you remain harm will come of it."

"I would not . . . wish to harm . . . His Lordship in . . . any way," Vanessa said gently.

"I can see you are a sensible girl," the Duchess said condescendingly. "If you will send me your address I will see that some small commissions come your way. The Dowager Countess of Clanderry, who lives in Berkeley Square, was saying only the other day that she wanted a portrait of her dog."

The Duchess paused and Vanessa knew she was expected to be grateful.

"Thank you, Ma'am," she murmured.

"But of course, I am relying on you to make your departure back to London with all possible speed," the Duchess continued.

She turned away towards the door. As she reached it she said:

"You may perhaps be wondering why I am particularly interested in the Marquis's good name. It is understood, and has been for many years, that His Lordship will marry my daughter, Lady Adelaide Wilmott, who is Lady-in-Waiting to Her Majesty the Queen. I am sure you appreciate, Miss Lens, why I would not wish there to be any unpleasant gossip about my future son-in-law."

The Duchess did not wait for Vanessa's reply but went from the Rose Drawing-Room and a footman closed the door behind her.

For some moments Vanessa did not move. Then she picked up the miniature which lay on the table, put it back in its frame, and hung it on the wall.

She packed her paints.

As she did, she knew that the Duchess had answered the question which had kept her awake all night, and there was in fact no longer a question to answer.

The arguments which had gone round and round in her brain and which she had thought so difficult to unravel were now quite simple.

She loved the Marquis and therefore she must not harm him.

There had been a condemnation and distaste in her voice as she had spoken which reminded Vanessa very forcibly of the way her mother had sometimes spoken in the past.

It was, she knew, what all real ladies felt about immorality; about women who offended the conventions; women who, whatever the excuses they might make, were nothing but wantons.

She saw now all too clearly the ugliness and degradation to which she had so nearly succumbed.

"That is not love," she told herself. "It is wicked and unclean."

It was something which she must never accept, even though it might tear her heart from her body to say no.

'I love . . . him! I love . . . him!' she thought despairingly.

But because of that love she ran quickly along the corridors and up the staircase to peal the bell in her bed-room for Dorcas.

Chapter Seven

"You have visited the pawn-shops?" the Marquis asked.

"Yes, M'Lord."

"And the Art Dealers—every one of them?"

"For the third time, M'Lord."

"Can you think of anywhere else we can possibly look?"

"I've made enquiries of the shops which might be patronised by the young lady—I've conversed with other shop-keepers in Islington—many of whom knew Miss Lens and her maid—but they've not seen either of them recently."

The Marquis looked down at a list of notes he had in front of him on his desk.

"You have tried the neighbourhoods adjacent to Islington?"

"All of them, M'Lord."

There was silence, then the Marquis said:

"As I have said before, no expense is to be spared. If you want more help and wish to engage assistants, do not hesitate to do so."

"I'm grateful for your permission, M'Lord, but there is in fact little that I've not done already. I can only continue to go on looking. The miniature you obtained for me is a great help."

The Marquis thought for a moment and then he said abruptly:

"Show me your account."

The man standing opposite him handed over a rather dirty piece of paper on which was written a sum of money.

The Marquis merely glanced at it and said:

"Take this to my secretary, Mr. Gratton. He will pay you what is owed and give you an extra amount in hand for your everyday expenses."

"Thank you, M'Lord! Thank you indeed!"

The middle-aged man, an ex-Bow Street Runner, bowed himself out of the room.

When he had gone the Marquis sat staring for a moment in front of him. Then he rose to walk to the window and look out onto the trees of the Square.

How was it possible, he asked himself, that someone could vanish so completely, as Vanessa had done?

For three weeks now he had been searching for her, employing every means at his disposal, but to no avail.

He could hardly believe that anyone, especially someone as young and inexperienced as Vanessa, could evade detection in a manner which left him puzzled and completely at a loss to know what to do next.

When he had returned to Ruckford Park, having dealt most effectively with the fire on the farm, it was later than he had intended.

It had required all his experience of organisation and leadership to calm down the farmer and his family; to get the animals to safety; and to prevent the fire from spreading any farther.

It was in fact entirely due to the manner in which the Marquis had taken control of the situation that the fire caused less damage than might otherwise have been expected.

But by the time the fire was out, scattered cattle rounded up, and accommodation allotted to the homeless family, the Marquis realised that he was nearly an hour late for luncheon.

He had, however, ridden back to Ruckford Park in a good humour.

It was pleasant to know that he had been instrumental in preventing the incident from developing into a disaster, and he was well aware that his employees had looked at him with admiration as well as gratitude when he had taken his farewell of them.

As he arrived at the front door a groom was waiting to take his horse and he walked quickly up the broad stone steps. Handing his hat to the Butler, he said:

"I am late, Jenkins! I hope Miss Lens did not wait luncheon for me."

"Miss Lens has left, M'Lord."

For a moment the meaning of the Butler's reply did not seem to penetrate the Marquis's mind. He had in fact started to walk towards the Dining-Room.

Then he stopped and asked:

"Left? What do you mean, left?"

"Miss Lens and her maid, M'Lord, departed for London at about eleven o'clock this morning."

"Departed for London?" the Marquis repeated almost stupidly.

"Miss Lens asked, M'Lord, if a carriage could convey her to where she intended to board the Stage-coach. But as she was in a hurry, I prevailed upon her to take the travelling carriage for the whole journey. I thought that would be Your Lordship's wish."

"Of course," the Marquis said quickly, "but why was Miss Lens in a hurry to return to London? Was there a message for her of any kind?"

"No, M'Lord, as far as I know Miss Lens received neither a message nor a letter."

"I do not understand," the Marquis said as if to himself.

"It did appear, M'Lord," the Butler continued, "that Miss Lens made up her mind to leave after she had spoken to Her Grace."

"Her Grace?" the Marquis questioned, and his voice was sharp.

"The Duchess of Tealby, M'Lord. Her Grace called and enquired for Your Lordship, and when she heard that you were not at home she asked to speak with Miss Lens."

The Marquis said nothing and after a moment the Butler continued:

"Miss Lens was in the Rose Drawing-Room, M'Lord. I understand she was doing some restoration work to one of Your Lordship's miniatures. Her Grace was with her for a short time and soon after she departed Miss Lens asked for a carriage to convey her to Beaconsfield."

The Marquis had drawn out his watch to look at it.

If Vanessa had left Ruckford Park at eleven o'clock she would by now, he reckoned, have reached London.

He decided to join her as soon as was possible, but he intended to visit the Duchess of Tealby first to discover what she had said to Vanessa.

He had a very good idea what that was. As usual, it infuriated him that anyone should interfere in his private affairs; moreover, the Duchess of Tealby was noted as a busy-body.

Having eaten quickly, he therefore changed his clothes and drove his phaeton to Tealby Castle.

There the Duchess at first received him effusively, only to freeze into an affronted coldness as the Marquis extracted from her more or less word for word what she had said to Vanessa.

"I cannot imagine, Ma'am," he said in a manner no less icy than the Duchess's, "why you should take it upon yourself to censure a young lady who was staying with me as my guest."

"I felt I had the right, Danien," the Duchess replied, "seeing that I have known you since you were in the cradle, and it was your father's earnest wish that our families should be united."

"It may have been my father's wish," the Marquis said, "but I am perfectly capable, Ma'am, of making up my own mind on matters that concern me personally."

"I am aware of that," the Duchess replied. "But there has never been a scandal at Ruckford Park, in my lifetime, and I cannot allow you to forfeit the respect in which the whole County holds you or damage the honoured name of your family."

"My family name has survived," the Marquis said with a sarcastic note in his voice, "generations of pirates, rakes, rogues, and spend-thrifts. If, as you say, I am respected in Oxfordshire, I cannot believe that my reputation is likely to be irretrievably damaged by inviting an extremely talented Artist into my home to oblige me by restoring my miniatures."

"She is too young and too pretty to be accepted at anything but her face-value," the Duchess snapped.

"That is something which would not have occurred to anyone had she not dined at Carlton House!" the Marquis retorted.

"I can see this conversation is getting us nowhere, Danien!" the Duchess said. "I can only beg of you to be more circumspect. No-one is concerned with what you do in London; but in the country, as you well know, things are different. I can only leave your future behaviour to your conscience!"

The Marquis had left Tealby Castle in a fury.

He was well aware that the Duchess's attitude was due not to any particular consideration for him or his good name, but merely to her inquisitive and interfering nature.

Her son, who was a stupid, rather irresponsible young man, had related to her what had occurred at Carlton House but had not, the Marquis was thankful to learn, included in his tattling the real reason for Vanessa's presence.

At the same time, it was quite obvious that by now the whole of the *Beau-Monde* would be asking why an unknown but extremely beautiful young girl had suddenly appeared and been invited at a moment's notice to His Royal Highness's table.

It was the sort of tit-bit of gossip that was bound to set tongues wagging, and the Marquis cursed the fact that it was impossible to do anything in the social world that was not shouted from the house-tops the following morning.

As he drove his horses towards London he made up his mind firmly and irrevocably that nothing would induce him to marry Lady Adelaide Wilmott.

She might make a commendable wife, but to have the Duchess for a mother-in-law was something which the Marquis decided he could not stomach.

In the future, he told himself, he would make very sure that the Duchess and any other women like her were not admitted to his house to make trouble amongst his guests when he was not present.

He only hoped that Vanessa would not be too distressed by what had been said.

He was well aware that the Duchess's strictness, coming on top of her fears of the night before, would have been disturbing.

Vanessa was so sensitive, so vulnerable, and so inexperienced that the Marquis realised that the last thing that should have happened was for her to be emotionally upset at this particular moment.

She was far too intelligent not to realise that the Duchess had been implying that she was his mistress, and he told himself it was particularly bad luck that he had not been at home when Her Grace had called.

He thought a little apprehensively as he neared London that he would have to be very gentle with Vanessa and not try to force her to make up her mind too quickly.

He was quite certain that eventually she would see sense and let him protect and look after her.

She loved him, and he wanted her so intensely that the sensations it aroused surprised him.

"I must not frighten her," he told himself when finally he drew his sweating team of horses to a standstill outside the little house in Islington.

The groom jumped down to hammer on the door and when it was not answered he knocked again.

As there continued to be no reply, the Marquis drove back to Berkeley Square to discover if his travelling carriage was there.

As he expected, the coachman was resting the horses before returning to Ruckford Park.

The Marquis sent for him.

"We did the journey in just under three hours, M'Lord!" the coachman reported, a note of satisfaction in his voice. "That was good timing," the Marquis agreed, "and you dropped Miss Lens at her home in Islington?"

"Yes, M'Lord, and the lady thanked me very prettily. I'm sure she enjoyed the drive."

"That will be all."

The man withdrew and after some light refreshment the Marquis once again drove to Islington with a fresh pair of horses.

The house was still bolted and barred.

This time the Marquis himself knocked on both doors and looked through the lower windows, but it was quite obvious that no-one was in the house.

He went round to the back and without much difficulty managed to open the window of the small room on the ground floor where Dorcas had slept.

He climbed in and started to systematically search the house.

When he entered the Sitting-Room, which, apart from the studio, was the only room he had seen, he noticed at once that the portrait of Vanessa's mother which had hung over the mantelshelf had gone!

There were also places on the walls where, he suspected, although he could not be certain, other pictures had been hanging.

There was a frown on his forehead as he walked upstairs, but he found nothing of value in any of the other rooms.

The whole place was furnished with good taste but the Marquis knew that the "break-up" value of the contents was little more than a few pounds.

He stood for a moment in Vanessa's small bed-room, and the white frill of the bed which matched the curtains and the frilled skirt of the dressing-table made him remember how exquisite she had looked the night before in her white evening-gown.

It was at that moment that he began to feel afraid that he might never find her again, and he had gone from the house knowing that the only clue to her whereabouts might be the picture of her mother.

He discovered it himself a week later. After visiting personally practically every Art Dealer in London, he saw the picture in a small shop in the city.

The dealer was only too willing to give the Marquis any information he required.

"Yes, I knew the late lamented Mr. Cornelius Lens, M'Lord. He was an excellent Artist and I've handled a number of his miniatures in my time."

"That is a picture of Mrs. Lens," the Marquis said, pointing to the portrait that had been hung on a wall beside two excrutiatingly badly executed watercolours of the Thames.

"Yes, indeed, M'Lord," the Dealer agreed. "A beautiful lady! I've often said to my wife: 'If Mrs. Lens had gone out into society like other Artists' wives, she would have caused a sensation!' but then she lived a very quiet life."

"The portrait was brought here by Miss Vanessa Lens. I am anxious to get in touch with her," the Marquis said. "Can you tell me her address?"

"She will be at her father's house in Islington, M'Lord."

"No, she is not there," the Marquis answered.

"Then I've no idea where she could be, M'Lord," the Dealer said. "She came in here two days ago with the picture."

"What did you give her for it?" the Marquis asked.

He saw the man hesitate and said sharply:

"I want the truth!"

"Eight guineas, M'Lord."

"Do you think that is all it is worth?"

"I doubt if I'll get more than twenty for it," the Dealer replied, "and I might have it on my hands for a long time. Cornelius Lens was well known for his miniatures, M'Lord. Those I can sell, but portraits of that sort are not in great demand."

"Did Miss Lens offer you anything else?" the Marquis asked.

"She had two framed drawings with her," the Dealer answered. "Not at all saleable, M'Lord; I bought them really out of charity."

"Let me see them," the Marquis ordered.

He realised when he looked at the drawings that they were extremely attractive sketches of Italian sculptures and he guessed that Cornelius Lens must have done them when he was abroad.

"How much did you pay for them?" he asked.

"Two guineas, M'Lord," the Dealer replied apologetically.

That meant, the Marquis thought, that Vanessa had only ten guineas with which to support herself and Dorcas, wherever they might be hiding.

He remembered only too vividly how she had admitted being worried about money, but had felt reassured by the fact that she had the Prince's miniatures and his own to work on.

Now the Marquis cursed himself for not having paid her for the work she had done. But he had been sure in his own mind that by the time she left Ruckford Park she would never have to worry about money again.

Ten pounds, ten shillings!

It was little enough, but he told himself optimistically that she would not have starved by the time he found her.

The Marquis bought the portrait of Mrs. Lens and the sketches from the Dealer, giving him the sums he asked on condition he promised to get in touch with him should Vanessa come into the shop again.

"You quite understand," he said authoritatively, "that if Miss Lens bring you anything to sell you are to buy it for a large sum, then explain that you have not so much money on you and ask her to call back later in the day. By that time you will have been able to send for me."

"I understand, M'Lord," the Dealer said.

He was so pleased with the sale of the pictures

that he would have been prepared to promise anything.

But the Marquis could not help feeling that sooner or later Vanessa would be obliged to return to Islington where at least she had a roof over her head.

He arranged with the ex-Bow Street Runner that the house would be watched and that if anyone called there he would be notified immediately.

The first few days after Vanessa's disappearance the Marquis passed in searching for her himself, feeling optimistic that he would find her.

Then he began to grow apprehensive.

For the first time in his life he found himself worrying over a woman, not because she had refused his advances but because he wanted to protect and shelter her from all that was hurtful and unpleasant.

He had never before in his life wanted to shield someone from unhappiness or to shoulder her burdens.

He would not have believed until he experienced it that the thought of Vanessa being alone in the world could torture him to the point when he felt at times he must go insane.

How could she possibly manage in London with only an old maid-servant to look after her when she was so lovely and so inexperienced?

He thought of men like Sir Julius Stone assaulting her, and he would rise from his bed to walk about the room clenching his fists together as if he were about to fight someone who dared to touch her.

He found himself imagining her in the most terrible and frightening situations without help; without anyone to hear her cries.

The scream she had given as he entered the studio echoed and reechoed in his ears until he could hear nothing else.

Every morning, rising earlier than he had ever done before, the Marquis rode not in the Park, as had been his wont, but in the streets, hoping that he might catch a glimpse of Dorcas or Vanessa going shopping, or merely walking in the quieter parts of North London or down by the river.

Sometimes he would see a figure that vaguely reminded him of Vanessa and his heart would give a leap as he spurred his horse forward eagerly, only to be disappointed.

As the days passed with no sign of her and the ex-Bow Street Runner only reiterated the same story of failure over and over again, the Marquis became frantic.

He called at all the Hospitals in case she might have had an accident, to be appalled at the conditions he found there but relieved that there was no sign of Vanessa there.

He visited Clergymen, asking if in their Congregations they had noticed either Vanessa or Dorcas, only to once again find himself frustrated and dismayed so that he spent another sleepless night walking the floor of his bed-room.

"You're losing a great deal of weight, M'Lord," his valet said to him. "Your coats are not fitting as well as they did."

"It is immaterial!" the Marquis remarked, and Jarvis looked at him in astonishment.

In all the years he had known His Lordship he had never known him not to be particular about his appearance.

It was after the third week since Vanessa's disappearance that the Marquis finally broke down and admitted to himself that he loved her as he had never loved a woman before.

He had never actually brought himself to say: 'I love you!' to any woman, and although he had told Vanessa that he wanted her he had never said the words 'I love you!' as she had said them to him.

Now he knew that this was love!

This agony, this pain, this ache within his heart was quite unlike any sensation that any woman had ever evoked in him before.

He had always believed that love was a delight; a delectation of the senses; a desire that could be assuaged and a passion which all too quickly faded.

What he felt for Vanessa was none of these things.

It was a need within himself that was as much

spiritual as it was physical. It was, in fact, the desire
of a man for a woman, not because she was beautiful
or exciting but because she was his whole heart and
soul.

"How can you do this to me, my darling?" he
asked aloud as he walked his bed-room floor in the
very early hours of the morning, and knew the true
answer was that he had done it to himself.

It was he who had swept away the radiance in
her face and the light from her eyes.

She had loved him and he had offered her not
love, but something she in her purity had known was
unclean.

For the first time in his life the Marquis saw himself as unprincipled and despicable.

He had found, he now realised, the most wonderful thing a man could ever discover, a pure and un-
spoilt love, and he had not understood the value of it.

He, who fancied himself a connoisseur, who
valued so highly the treasures he had collected and
those which he had inherited from his ancestors, had
not recognised a pearl of great price even when he
had it in his grasp.

"Fool! Fool! Fool!" he cried aloud into the darkness, and knew that never again would he know happiness until he found Vanessa.

It seemed impossible that the days could drag by
so slowly or that he, who had always been successful
in obtaining everything he wanted, should find,
whichever way he turned, whichever way he looked,
nothing but failure.

He had been so certain when he borrowed Cor-
nelius Lens's miniature of his daughter from the
Prince of Wales that it would be easy for the ex-Bow
Street Runner to find her.

But even this had brought forth no results, and
the Marquis resorted to visiting places where he
thought Vanessa might go in search of cheap goods.

There were paints and other Artists' materials to
be found in the Pantheon Bazaar and he went there
himself, much to the curiosity of the women shopping
for lengths of material or straw bonnets.

He walked down small streets where the grocers cut their prices to attract customers and even talked with barrow-traders who sold oysters and whelks, the men who hawked fresh carrots from the country, and the women who cried their fruit.

Where could Vanessa be?

It seemed to the Marquis that he was up against a wall which he could neither break through nor scale.

His friends, not unnaturally, thought it extraordinary that he attended none of the parties to which he was invited, nor was he to be found at White's or any of the gaming Clubs they frequented in the evening.

The House of Lords saw him briefly when his attendance was important, but otherwise he was endlessly searching for Vanessa, worrying about her and becoming, he admitted to himself, more and more desperate.

The Prince of Wales, having been told of the Marquis's unusual behaviour, was determined to find out the reason for it.

He sent the Marquis a note inviting him to dine with him the following evening and proceed after dinner to Vauxhall Gardens, where he wished to view a new attraction—a night balloon.

His Royal Highness couched the letter in such terms that it was practically a Royal Command and impossible for the Marquis to refuse.

He therefore accepted to dine at Carlton House with a somewhat ill grace which was not assuaged when on arrival he was submitted to what was essentially a cross-questioning as to his recent activities.

Fortunately, the Prince was seldom interested in anyone but himself for long, and his attention quickly veered from the Marquis towards some valuable acquisitions he had added to his collection.

There were many of the Marquis's personal friends at dinner and he found himself relaxing and enjoying the intelligent conversation even while at the back of his thoughts there was always the aching need for Vanessa.

Finally when dinner was finished they set off for supper at Vauxhall.

The famous gardens, which had been a place of amusement for many years, had been greatly improved in 1728 by a new owner, Jonathan Tyers.

Hogarth, who lived close by, had suggested he should reopen the gardens with a grand *ridotto al fresco*, the main attraction being the embellishment of the Pavilions in the gardens by the famous Artist himself.

Hogarth's pictures of Henry VIII and Ann Boleyn were placed in the Rotunda and he allowed Francis Hayman to copy his *Four Times of the Day*.

The pictures, which were gay, amusing, and brilliant in colour, added to the attraction of the alcoves furnished in Eastern style and brought many new visitors to the gardens.

Tyers also erected a statue of Handel and increased the illuminations so that five thousand oil-lamps made Vauxhall one of the brightest places in London.

But this was very small-fry compared with the fourteen thousand lamps that were lit at Vauxhall towards the end of the century, when every year more ambitious attractions drew the crowds which included the Prince of Wales and his friends.

The Prince had his own Pavilion with its private entrance to the road. In the centre of the grove the ornate double-fronted band-stand, which looked like a Chinese pagoda and housed the musicians, was surmounted by the Prince of Wales's feathers.

Round the Rotunda in a great semi-circle was a range of alcoves or Pavilions, as they were called, used as supper-boxes, each one furnished with a table and six or seven chairs.

Every supper-box contained a painting by Hayman and they owed their names to the subject depicted in the painting.

There was "The Dragon," "The King's Head," "The Royal Arbour," "The Ship," and "The Royal George."

The Marquis, who had visited Vauxhall many times, found himself bored at the prospect of listening once again to the singing of a *Prima Donna* whom he knew he could hear in greater comfort in the Opera-House.

He was not interested in the slices of the famous "Vauxhall Ham" for which the proprietor charged an outrageous price.

It was boasted that the carvers could cut enough wafer-like slices from one ham to cover the whole eleven acres of the garden!

But as the Prince was determined to enjoy himself, the Marquis felt he could not be so churlish as to refuse to take part in the festivities.

His Royal Highness and his party were received by Mr. C. H. Simpson, the Master of Ceremonies, who was a great character.

Wearing silk hose, knee breeches, cut-away suit, and beaver-hat, he was small and bald-headed, but he was a lover of *panache* and bore, as a rod of office, a silver-headed cane with the utmost pomposity.

"Some people describe him as 'that kind, smiling idiot,'" the Prince remarked to the Marquis in an audible aside.

The profusion of coloured lamps imitating flowers, the brilliance of the music, the trees beaded with ornaments, and the noise and laughter of the crowds gave an impression of wild gaiety.

Fireworks were a familiar attraction at Vauxhall. The whole air would be ablaze with crowns, hearts, initials, and figures in meteoric flashes. But the night-balloon was to be something quite original.

The Marquis remembered there had been a great deal of talk when the same French aeronaut, Monsieur Garnerin, had, two years earlier, tested his new invention of a parachute.

As he had not liked to risk his own life until he was sure the parachute would work, he had hitched his unfortunate cat to the apparatus and launched it from the balloon down towards the gardens.

The cat luckily arrived safely to inspire column upon column of controversy in the newspapers.

After that, Garnerin had condescended to try out the parachute for himself and it landed him quite safely near St. Pancras Church.

Now he intended to exhibit a night-balloon and the idea had taken the fancy of the Prince.

"I imagine we are going to see nothing we have not seen before," the Marquis murmured to the Duchess of Devonshire.

She smiled at him and replied:

"As we grow older we enjoy child-like things."

Then at the expression on his face she asked quietly:

"What is wrong with you, Danien? I have never before known you so down-at-the-mouth."

"I will tell you sometime," he answered, "but not now." .

"You have changed," she said. "You have grown thinner, for one thing, and I have never seen you before without that proud air of supremacy, as if the whole world lay subservient beneath your feet."

The Marquis was surprised that she was so perceptive, but as he had always liked the Duchess he said:

"As it happens, for the first time in my life I am desperately worried."

"Can it be possible," she enquired, "that some unique female has refused you?"

He did not answer and after a moment she said quietly:

"I will not tease you. I am sorry if all is not well and I hope that in the future everything will come right."

"I can only pray it will!" the Marquis said with a note of sincerity in his voice which surprised the Duchess.

As they were talking the bell had rung from the Rotunda to announce that the exhibition was about to take place. The Marquis rose and walked towards the crowd that was gathering from all parts of the garden onto the lawn in front of the band-stand.

In the centre of it was the brilliantly lit balloon which Monsieur Garnerin was ready to launch into the sky.

It looked to the Marquis very like all other balloons. He had seen several launched in Hyde Park and even in childhood he had been taken to see Vincent

Lunardis when it was on display in the Pantheon in 1784.

But he was well aware that everyone round him was exceedingly excited by its brilliant colour and floating pennants.

The guests in the Pavilions, with glasses of wine in their hands, were straining forward to watch and the orchestra was playing spirited music which seemed somehow to be in keeping with the adventurous spirit of the occasion.

The balloon was released amidst the cheers of the crowd and it ascended with unexpected velocity.

When it had reached a considerable height above the gardens, the fireworks attached to it went off, showering a stream of gold, red, and blue lights down towards the upturned faces.

The Marquis found himself yawning.

He started to move back towards the Royal Pavilion, but the crowds made it difficult for him to push his way through them and he turned once again to look up at the balloon.

Now the fireworks had set the balloon itself on fire and it was a burning ball in the darkness of the sky.

"Do you know what she said to me?" a woman beside him remarked to her friend. "She said, 'If you look in his eye you will be able to see if he loves you'!"

There was a light laugh.

"Did she mean the real eye, or the one she had painted?"

"The one she had painted, of course. That was why I paid five shillings for it. At the same time, there may be something in what she says."

"You are just being credulous, Letty."

The Marquis had listened to the conversation with only part of his mind, then suddenly he was alert!

He turned to look at the two ladies beside him. Expensively gowned, they were, he could see, gentleborn and were not alone but escorted by two gentlemen.

In the hand of the first woman who had spoken the Marquis could see a piece of paper. He swept his hat from his head.

"Forgive me, Ma'am," he said, "but I heard you mention that you had bought a painting of an eye. Would you be gracious enough to tell me where you obtained it?"

The woman to whom he was speaking looked at him a little apprehensively and he realised that she was on her guard against being accosted by a strange man in Vauxhall Gardens.

Then as if the Marquis's elegant appearance reassured her she replied:

"It is a new enterprise for Vauxhall, Sir; a Persian Artist in the last arbour of the Rotunda will paint a person's eye for the sum of five shillings."

She held out the piece of paper for the Marquis to see.

He looked down at it and saw that even though it was in fact only a rough outline of an eye with the pupil uncoloured, it was exceedingly well executed.

"The last arbour of the Rotunda," he repeated. "Thank you very much, Ma'am, for your information."

He bowed and walked quickly in the direction of the Rotunda.

His boredom and lassitude had vanished and he felt as if he had suddenly come alive! Every nerve in his body was tingling with anticipation.

Side-shows had never been permitted at Vauxhall, and yet at the end of the Rotunda, where every Pavilion was filled with people eating and drinking, the last alcove had been curtained off.

Outside it there was a notice which read:

> Madame Shahriza, the Persian Seer, will
> paint a lucky eye for those who would
> seek good fortune and love.

As the Marquis read the notice the curtains parted and a man and a woman came out from the alcove, giggling together.

"It'll bring us luck! I know it'll bring us luck!" the woman said excitedly.

"As long as I can look into your eyes," the man replied, "I've no wish to stare at a piece of paper!"

The woman made some retort but the Marquis, without waiting to listen, parted the curtains and entered the alcove.

What had originally been a small supper-room had been made smaller by a table set in the centre of it.

Behind it sat a woman with her head heavily veiled and wearing a yashmak. It covered the whole of her face with the exception of her eyes.

These were, however, in shadow, owing to the fact that two oil-lamps placed at each end of the table were shaded at the back so that the light shone only to the front and left Madame Shahriza almost in darkness.

On the table were pieces of thick paper cut into squares, an Artist's palette, brushes, and several pencils.

The Persian Artist was drawing on one of the pieces of paper as the Marquis entered. She did not look up but merely said:

"Will you seat yourself on the chair with the light on your face?"

The Marquis walked forward and obeyed.

The Artist finished the outline of an eye and looked up. She gave a visible start and her long thin fingers were still.

"I would like you to look into my eye," the Marquis said.

There was silence and he knew that Vanessa was finding it impossible to speak.

After a moment he said quietly:

"How could you have hidden yourself here? You have driven me crazy these past weeks!"

She did not answer and he added:

"We cannot talk here. Get your cloak, Vanessa. My carriage is outside."

He thought she would argue, but as if she re-

alised that it was hopeless she rose slowly from the
table. Her hands were trembling as she put first her
palette and then the pieces of paper into a box which
contained her paints.

The Marquis watched her. When at length she
turned back to pick up her cloak which was in the
shadows behind her he rose to put it round her shoulders.

"Surely you are not alone?" he asked.

For the first time Vanessa spoke.

"Dorcas . . . always comes with . . . me," she answered, "but tonight she was not well . . . I insisted on
her . . . staying behind."

"Then I will take you back to her," the Marquis
said.

They walked from the alcove into the crowds
who were still staring at what remained of the burning balloon. Now it looked only like a small piece of
paper flaring against the sky.

The Marquis put his hand under Vanessa's arm
and drew her towards the Water-Gate which was a
public entrance not far from the Prince's Pavilion.

They walked outside to where the Marquis's carriage was waiting behind the Royal Carriages at the
head of a long row of vehicles which stretched down
the whole length of Kennington Lane.

At the sight of His Lordship his footman sprang
down from the box and opened the door. Vanessa
stepped inside and the Marquis followed her.

"Where do you wish to go?" he asked.

"Number twelve Museum Lane," she answered in
a low voice.

The Marquis gave the man the address and the
carriage started off.

Slowly, with hands that were trembling, Vanessa
pushed back the hood which had covered her head
and undid the yashmak which had obscured her face.

She looked up at the Marquis and he could see by
the light of the lantern in the carriage that her eyes
were dark and troubled.

For a moment he could only stare at her, his eyes
on her pale face.

"You . . . have been . . . looking for . . . me?" she asked.

"I have searched for you from one end of London to the other!" the Marquis replied. "How could you do anything so cruel? So utterly and completely damnable as to leave me like that?"

"It was . . . doing you . . . harm for me to stay at . . . Ruckford Park."

"You mean you were thinking only of me?"

"Y-yes, and . . . also I . . . could not . . . do as you . . . asked."

"You were right to decide that," the Marquis said. "It was something I had no right to ask of you, and I am ashamed, bitterly and humbly ashamed, Vanessa, of my behaviour."

He saw the surprise in her eyes. Then as if he could not help himself he reached out and took her hands in his.

"Oh, my darling!" he said, and his voice broke. "Say you will marry me, for I swear that I cannot live without you."

He knew that Vanessa stiffened with surprise. Then she said in a whisper:

"Why are you . . . now asking me to . . . m-marry you?"

"Because I love you!" the Marquis answered. "Because I love you as I never thought it possible to love anyone; because by leaving as you did, you tortured and nearly destroyed me, Vanessa; because I know now that all I want of life is for you to be with me and that you should be my wife!"

She looked at him in sheer astonishment.

"But I . . . t-thought . . ." she stammered after a moment, "you were to . . . m-marry . . . s-someone else."

"I am to marry no-one but you, Vanessa. I could not contemplate any other woman as my wife."

He saw a light come to her eyes and an almost incredible radiance transform her face.

Then as if it was inevitable his arms went round her and he sought her lips.

He kissed her at first very gently, keeping a tight control of himself in case he should frighten her.

Until, as he felt her lips soft and yielding beneath his and something wonderful and ecstatic enveloped them with the same magic they had known on the terrace at Ruckford Park, his lips became more insistent, more passionate, and more demanding.

He held her so close that she could hardly breathe and when at length he raised his head she thought even in the candlelight that he looked different from the way he had ever looked before.

"I love you! God, how I love you! Forgive me, Vanessa, forgive me for what I suggested, for insulting you, for not realising, because I was such a fool, that the love we have for each other is the most marvellous, the most precious thing a man could ever know."

"Are you . . . really saying . . . this to . . . me?" Vanessa whispered.

"I love you, my darling, but until I lost you I was so thick-headed that I did not understand what you meant to me. Now I have found you; now we are together and everything will be completely and absolutely perfect!"

His lips sought hers again and he kissed her until she felt as if he carried her up to the sky where there were only the stars and an ecstasy that was not of this world.

Finally when the Marquis knew they were drawing near to the British Museum he said:

"I have a Special Licence, my sweet love—will you marry me tomorrow?"

"T-tomorrow?"

Vanessa repeated the word as if it was hard to speak, and he knew by the radiance in her face that it was difficult for her to think of anything except that she was in his arms.

"You are beautiful!" he said softly, "more beautiful than I remember. But, my precious, have you been safe?"

He pushed back the veiling that had covered

her hair and the gold of it, with its shimmer of red, lit the darkness.

He touched it with gentle hands. Then he lifted her chin once again so that her lips were near to his.

"Tell me," he said in his deep voice, "if you have missed me?"

"Without . . . you I . . . wanted to . . . die!"

"My poor little love! My darling!"

"But I had to look after . . . Dorcas . . . she is not well . . . and she does not . . . like the boarding-house where we are staying."

"I shall take you away first thing in the morning," the Marquis promised. "Or could you leave tonight?"

"We could not . . . move Dorcas."

"No, I understand that. But you have not answered my question. You have been safe?"

She nodded her head.

"It was . . . frightening at times, but Dorcas . . . looked after me and I had some . . . money."

"I know that," the Marquis answered. "Your mother's portrait is waiting for you in my house."

"Oh, I am glad!" she exclaimed. "I did not wish to lose it."

"No more than I wished to lose you!" the Marquis added. "Why did you go to Vauxhall? It was the last place I would have thought of looking for you."

"Papa had once been asked to restore one of Hayman's pictures, which had been damaged during a fight in an arbour," Vanessa answered. "Mr. Simpson came to call after the work was completed.

"When I went to see him three weeks ago and told him that I had to make some money, he was kind enough to suggest I should use one of the arbours and paint the portrait of an eye for those who were prepared to pay for it."

"It was a clever idea," the Marquis said, "but not for you, my darling, not for you!"

"No-one could see my face, which was why I wore a yashmak, and Mr. Simpson lent me the money to buy the rest of my costume."

"It was a sensible disguise," the Marquis approved, "but I cannot bear to think of your going to the gardens every night; leaving yourself open to the attentions of strange men."

"I think most . . . people were . . . afraid of me in case I put the . . . 'evil eye' on them," Vanessa said with a faint smile.

"It was brave of you, my dearest love, but too brave. Now that I have found you again there will be no more fears and difficulties, no more unhappiness. And as far as I am concerned, no more agonising nights when I could not sleep for wondering where you were."

"Have you really been . . . worrying so much . . . about me?"

He smiled at the absurdity of the question, remembering the tortures he had suffered.

"Let us forget it," he replied. "Tomorrow you will be my wife and we will be happy together for the rest of our lives."

Vanessa looked away from him and he added anxiously:

"You will marry me?"

"I am . . . not . . . sure."

"What do you mean?"

"I have thought so . . . often of what you . . . said to me! You told me that your title and position entailed certain . . . obligations and that you could only marry . . . someone whose family equalled your own in rank and importance."

"I was talking sheer rubbish!" the Marquis exclaimed angrily. "I was conceited, puffed up with my own consequence, and altogether abominable, Vanessa! You are to forget everything I said. I despise myself for being so bird-witted and idiotic!"

Vanessa smiled as if she could not help it.

"You are very harsh with yourself."

"I mean every word," the Marquis retorted almost savagely. "If you will marry me, Vanessa, I shall be the luckiest, the most fortunate man in the world. No-one could have a more perfect or more beautiful wife! The only thing is, I am convinced that I do not deserve you!"

"It is so . . . wonderful that you should . . . say such things to . . . me," she murmured.

At the same time, he sensed that there was still a shadow in her eyes.

"Darling, we can talk about all this tomorrow," he said. "But let me make this quite clear: I intend to make you my wife and nothing and nobody shall stop me! I know now what it is like to live without you, and I could not contemplate the years ahead if you were not at my side."

He spoke with such forceful sincerity that Vanessa could not help believing him, and yet she said hesitatingly:

"Because I . . . love you, I shall not . . . wish to . . . harm you in . . . any way. That is why I . . . left Ruckford Park."

"I know that," the Marquis said, "and if any interfering busy-body old woman tries to make trouble between us in the future, I promise you she will get short-shift. You are mine, Vanessa, mine, as you always have been from the moment we first met each other!"

His arms tightened round her and he went on:

"Fate brought us together and, having lost you, thanks to fate I have found you again. Please, my darling, marry me, unless you wish me to be utterly and abjectly miserable."

He spoke so beguilingly that instinctively Vanessa moved closer to him, her face uplifted to his.

His lips took possession of her and it was with the greatest difficulty that they realised that the carriage had come to a standstill.

Reluctantly, as the footman opened the door, the Marquis took his arms away.

"Until tomorrow, my beloved!" he said.

He saw the happiness in her face as she looked up at him before she turned to alight from the carriage.

The Marquis followed her onto the pavement.

He saw that they were outside one of the tall, dilapidated buildings in a lane off the British Museum which had been turned into a cheap boarding-house.

He could not bear to think of Vanessa living in such a place or having such a sordid background.

He wanted to carry her away there and then to Ruckford House and make quite certain that she was safe and comfortable. But then he knew that it would upset her, and she would never agree to leave Dorcas or try to move her when the old woman was ill.

"I shall call for you at eleven o'clock tomorrow," he said. "Will that be time enough for you to do your packing?"

"I have not much to pack," Vanessa smiled.

"Eleven o'clock, then," he said. "Until then, my perfect little love, I leave my heart in your keeping."

He raised her hands to his lips and she felt the warm insistence of his mouth against her skin and a little quiver of delight run through her because once again he was touching her.

Then because words were so inadequate she moved away from him into the house.

She ran up the dusty stairs, lifting her skirts as she did so, and reached the third floor as if there were wings on her feet.

She opened the door of the small, low-ceilinged bed-room which she shared with Dorcas, with its two iron bedsteads and peeling wall-paper.

Dorcas was awake lying back against the pillows, a candle beside her bed.

Vanessa burst into the room and shut the door behind her.

"Oh, Dorcas! Dorcas!"

"What is it? What's happened?"

"He found me! His Lordship found me!" Vanessa said, her voice a paean of joy. "He loves me, Dorcas, and he has asked me to marry him! He has a Special Licence. How can I refuse him, even though I know I should do so?"

"He has asked you to marry him, Miss Vanessa?" Dorcas asked.

"He has begged me to do so! He wants me as I want him—more than anything else in the world!"

Dorcas gave a deep sigh that seemed to come from the very depths of her old body.

"Thank God! Thank God, Miss Vanessa! My prayers have been answered!"

Chapter Eight

The Marquis walked into Ruckford House with an expression on his face which made his footmen look at him apprehensively.

They knew their Master was blue-devilled, but they thought that they had never seen him look quite so darkly unapproachable as he was at that moment.

Having given his hat and gloves to the Butler without speaking, the Marquis proceeded to the Library where he flung himself down on a chair and rested his chin on his hand.

A few minutes later the door opened and the Butler said in an apologetic voice:

"Alfonse has been waiting, M'Lord, to know if there is anything you wish to eat."

"Nothing!" the Marquis replied.

"May I suggest something light and palatable, M'Lord? You have not eaten to my knowledge for twenty-four hours!"

"I am not hungry!"

"It's a mistake, if I may say so, M'Lord, to fast for so long."

"Leave me alone!"

There was nothing the Butler could do but obey orders and he closed the door quietly behind him.

The Marquis sat staring with unseeing eyes across the room.

It seemed to him completely impossible that Vanessa should have disappeared again.

The previous day he had arrived in Museum Lane as he had arranged, at eleven o'clock. He was driving his own phaeton, in which he intended to convey Vanessa to Berkeley Square. It was followed by a carriage for Dorcas and the luggage.

The Marquis had arranged with the Vicar of St. George's Hanover Square that they should be married by Special Licence immediately after luncheon.

The Parson would be waiting for them and the Marquis had already given orders for the Altar to be decorated with white flowers.

It would be a quiet ceremony, but he knew that that was what Vanessa and he himself would like best.

He had no desire to subject her on their wedding-day to the curiosity and inevitably the criticism of his social friends.

The fact that his marriage would cause a great deal of surprise was something the Marquis faced quite frankly.

He knew that, when he had avoided matrimony for so long, after being pursued by a variety of ambitious and distinguished parents, the fact that he had chosen to marry someone obscure and with slightly dubious antecedents would inevitably evoke much unfavourable comment.

He minded for Vanessa's sake, but he did not care in the slightest as far as he himself was concerned.

His love for Vanessa had swept away all his snobbery and vanity; the only thing he wanted was to make her happy, as he knew she would be once they were together.

It was unfortunate, he reflected, that Artists in general, and Miniaturists in particular were in somewhat bad odour with the social world.

The ridiculous pretensions of Richard Cosway

and the scandalously loose life he led had not escaped the notice of those who would accept raffish behaviour from members of their own class, but not from those they considered beneath them.

Artists had been accepted as loose-livers since the beginning of time, and people thought little of it; but the Prince of Wales, in making Cosway his friend and being seen frequently in his company, had forced him upon the social world.

In consequence, Cosway's private life was brought to the attention of the *Beau-Monde*.

"It does not matter to me," the Marquis told himself. "Vanessa is different and her father apparently lived in an exemplary manner."

The same, however, could not be said of her grandfather, Peter Paul Lens. But his expulsion from Ireland and the devil-worship in which he had indulged in the Hellfire Club would, the Marquis hoped, be unknown in London.

Nevertheless, there was no disguising the fact that there were difficulties ahead and he must be prepared to fight an increasing battle to protect his wife from the snubs and slights which the great social hostesses would be only too ready to inflict on her.

The Marquis knew, however, that he had some close friends on whom he could rely: the Duchess of Devonshire was one and the Countess of Bessborough another.

Moreover, he knew that the Prince of Wales would support him whatever he did or whomever he married.

He had therefore gone to collect Vanessa from the Bloomsbury boarding-house at peace within himself and filled with a strange, unworldly happiness that he had never known before.

He could not believe he was hearing aright when the proprietress, a blowsy woman with a somewhat aggressive manner, informed him that Vanessa and her maid had already left.

"I do not believe you!" the Marquis exclaimed.

The woman had merely laughed in his face.

"Go up and look for y'self, me fine gentleman!" she jeered. "Third floor back, and if your lady-friend 'as left it untidy, don't blame me!"

Because the Marquis was certain that she must be lying, he had climbed to the third floor and found, as he had been told, an empty room.

He looked at the two iron bedsteads, the peeling wall-paper, and the bare floor with disgust and horror.

He could not imagine Vanessa, so lovely and so perfect in herself, in such a place.

Then he remembered that she had stayed here rather than in her own house simply because she believed that she was harming him in becoming a part of his life.

He had then driven from Museum Lane to Islington, thinking that Vanessa must have gone home feeling, as he did, that the boarding-house was not the right background from which to set out on a new life.

The house in Islington was, however, exactly as he had last seen it.

The doors were locked and barred, the windows closed, and although the Marquis let himself into the house he could not see that anything else had been removed.

Once again he found himself calculating desperately how much money Vanessa would have left.

It was true that she must have made a certain amount at Vauxhall but, although she had not told him so, he was certain that Mr. Simpson, being a business-man, would have charged her rent for the arbour.

Out of her earnings she would also undoubtedly have given him something towards what she owed for the Persian gown and veils with which she had disguised herself.

The Marquis had driven quickly back to Berkeley Square, trying to make himself believe that Vanessa had left the boarding-house intending to come direct to him.

There was, however, no sign of her!

All through the day he had searched frantically in

every part of London where he thought she might be hiding.

Although he had known it was hopeless, he had that evening gone to Vauxhall Gardens, only to find the arbour empty and Mr. Simpson without the slightest idea of why she had not turned up as he had expected.

The Marquis spent a sleepless, tormented night, walking about his bed-room and haunted by the words he had said to Vanessa and which had made her hesitate to agree to marry him.

"How could I ever have been so incredibly pompous," he asked himself, "so absurdly conceited, apart from the fact that I was insulting her?"

He knew at this moment that he would sacrifice his rank and his entire fortune just to hold Vanessa in his arms and persuade her, as he himself was persuaded, that nothing else mattered except their love.

"I love you! I love you!" he wanted to say to her as she had said it to him.

Yet he could see, as if it were etched indelibly on his memory, the expression on her face, from which the radiance had vanished, when he told her he could not offer her marriage!

Today he had started once again to comb London, visiting Dealers, shops, and boarding-houses, and he had returned to Ruckford House only because his horse was tired.

Sitting in the Library, he tried to think of somewhere new he could go, but he was aware that it was only by chance that he had found Vanessa before, and a lucky number seldom turned up twice running when one was gambling.

The door opened behind the Marquis and Mr. Gratton came into the room.

"Excuse me, My Lord," he said, "but a note has just been delivered at the door and the groom says it is urgent!"

The Marquis sat upright with a glint of hope in his eyes.

"A note?" he asked.

"It is from the Dowager Countess of Clanderry, My Lord."

The Marquis sank back again in the chair and his expression was once again one of despair.

As he did not speak or attempt to take the note that Mr. Gratton was holding, his secretary asked after a moment:

"Shall I open it, My Lord?"

"It cannot be anything important," the Marquis replied.

Taking this as permission to see what the note contained, Mr. Gratton lifted the wafer and spread out the note on which there was writing in an elegant, female hand.

Mr. Gratton glanced through it, then read aloud:

"The Dowager Countess of Clanderry presents her compliments to the Marquis of Ruckford and asks him to call on her this afternoon at five o'clock on a matter which is of the utmost import."

Mr. Gratton's voice died away and when there was no response from the Marquis he said:

"The groom said it was urgent, M'Lord."

"Tell her to go to the devil!" the Marquis replied savagely.

There was silence. Then Mr. Gratton said quietly:

"I think that would be a mistake, My Lord, if you will forgive me for saying so. The Countess, as Your Lordship knows, is a neighbour, and perhaps this is an olive-branch after so many years of complaints and opposition."

The Marquis did not speak and after a moment Mr. Gratton added:

"She was, I understand, My Lord, a close friend of both Your Lordship's mother and your father."

The Marquis sighed.

"Very well then," he said ungraciously, "have it your own way, Gratton. Inform the groom that I will call on Her Ladyship at five o'clock, but God knows what she wants of me!"

"It is already nearly half after four, My Lord," Mr. Gratton said as he turned towards the door.

Scowling and with a bad grace, the Marquis went upstairs to change his clothes.

He knew he would not dare present himself to the Dowager Countess in riding-breeches.

It was true, as Mr. Gratton had said, that the Dowager had been a friend of both his father and mother, but she had made it clear that she disapproved of him from the moment he became a companion and friend of the Prince of Wales.

There were just a few great hostesses in London who not only voiced their disapproval of the Prince, but also would not invite him into their houses if he was accompanied by Mrs. Fitzherbert.

As the Prince refused every invitation unless Mrs. Fitzherbert was also invited, this meant that there was a small social clique who censured him with some severity.

They were, however, *persona grata* at Buckingham Palace, and the Dowager Countess of Clanderry was frequently in attendance upon the Queen.

The Prince laughed and sneered at those who would not entertain him; but at the same time, the Marquis knew, it was a thorn in his flesh to know that he was not welcomed by some of his father's most distinguished subjects.

As the Marquis's valets assisted him to change into one of his most elegant coats and tied his cravat in an intricate pattern which could be achieved by few of the Dandies, he attempted to recall what the Dowager Countess looked like.

He had not seen her since his father died, but he remembered that she was stiff-necked, straight-backed, and was the type of *grande dame* with whom the Prince and his rollicking friends would have nothing in common.

At the same time, the Marquis rather respected the stand that the Dowager Countess and two or three other great ladies had taken against the behaviour and extravagance of Carlton House, and most of all against the Prince's flaunting of the conventions by foisting his mistress upon the social world.

When finally the Marquis walked downstairs his carriage was waiting at the door and it was a few minutes to five o'clock.

The Dowager Countess's house was only at the other side of the Square but it would have been insulting, the Marquis knew, to arrive on foot when he was calling on a lady who had closed her doors against him for at least eight years.

He was interested as he entered the formal marble Hall to see a fine portrait of one of the Earls of Clanderry painted by Van Dyck.

On the stairs as he climbed towards the Drawing-Room there was an even better Rubens than he himself had recently purchased from Lord Hargrave.

The Marquis had time to examine it, as the retainer who led the way was extremely old and it seemed as if even the enormous silver-crested buttons on his livery were almost too much for him to carry.

Breathless when he reached the top of the stairs, he however managed to announce the Marquis in stentorian tones.

"The Marquis of Ruckford, M'Lady!"

The Marquis, entering the long, narrow Drawing-Room, saw at the far end of it a fragile figure with grey hair seated by a window.

He walked slowly towards the Dowager Countess and when he reached her side she rose stiffly to extend towards him a blue-veined hand, which he raised perfunctorily to his lips.

"Your servant, Ma'am!" he said, making her a bow which was unequalled in elegance.

"Pray be seated, My Lord," the Dowager Countess said formally.

Her voice, as he had expected, was cold and somewhat austere, and, he fancied, had a note of disapproval in it.

The Marquis sat down, deciding as he did so that the Dowager Countess must wish to speak to him about the Square.

Various battles had been conducted through their secretaries over the past years regarding the upkeep of the garden in the centre, the parking of the carriages, the noise at nights, and the behaviour of linkmen, the Dowager invariably complaining about those employed by the Marquis.

The Dowager Countess, having seated herself, as the Marquis had expected, erect and straight-backed, looked at him, he thought, with shrewd eyes, as if she was searching for something, although he had not the slightest idea what it might be.

She must have been very beautiful in her youth. Her hair was now dead white but it was still profuse, and despite the many lines and wrinkles on her face her features were fine-cut and classical, while her bone-structure would have been the delight of any portrait-painter.

"You are perhaps surprised, My Lord, that I have asked you to call upon me and at short notice," the Dowager Countess began after a moment.

"It is certainly a long time since we met, Ma'am," the Marquis replied.

"As you well know," the Dowager went on, "I admired your father and was extremely fond of your mother, but I disapprove of those with whom you choose to associate."

"I can only express my regret, Ma'am, if it has troubled you in any way," the Marquis replied.

"It has been of little consequence to me!" the Dowager Countess said coldly. "But on moral and social grounds I will not receive the Prince of Wales so long as he consorts with that Mrs. Fitzherbert, and the fact that it is now rumoured he has morganatically married her in my opinion only makes the situation far worse!"

"I would agree with you, Ma'am, if it were true," the Marquis remarked.

"We can only hope that for the sake of the Throne it is a falsehood!" the Dowager Countess said. "However, I have not brought you here to speak about the Prince, even though I could say a great deal on the subject!"

The Marquis waited and after a moment the Dowager Countess continued:

"You know the history of my husband's family, I think. The O'Derry's were Kings of Ireland far back into the annals of time."

"I am aware of that, Ma'am," the Marquis said in what he hoped was a tone of respect.

"The Earldom dates from the Twelfth Century," the Dowager Countess went on as if he had not spoken. "Yours, I believe, was created in the Seventeenth."

"Sixteen fifty-five, to be precise!"

"While your Marquisate is of more recent origin . . ."

"Seventeen twenty-two!"

The Marquis wondered to what all this appertained, but he did not wish to interrupt even though he hoped that sooner rather than later the Dowager Countess would come to the point of her summons.

"My husband, the Nineteenth Earl, was, as you can expect, very proud of his antecedents."

"Of course, Ma'am."

The Marquis knew that many people had a fixation about genealogical trees and the way their family had bred and expanded all down the ages.

While he was proud of being blue-blooded, he had seldom worried about his ancestors save where they concerned himself. But he did know that the O'Derrys were one of the oldest and proudest of the Irish aristocracy.

"You will therefore understand," the Dowager Countess went on, "that my husband, having five sons and only one daughter, should insist that she married well."

The Marquis looked at his hostess in perplexity.

Surely, he thought, this was not a preamble to some suggestion of marriage?

"He therefore chose from, I may say, quite a number of suitors the man he considered the most fitting for my daughter, Elizabeth."

The Dowager Countess paused before she added:

"I do not think it ever occurred to him that my

daughter would oppose his wishes in any way or refuse to accept the husband he was prepared to accept as his son-in-law."

She gave a little sigh.

"Even now, all these years later, I cannot imagine how I was so blind that I did not see what was happening under my very nose! But I suppose I never expected to find a rebel in my midst, and certainly not my one and only daughter!"

There was a note of pain in the old voice, and the Marquis looked at the Dowager Countess in surprise.

He still could not guess what this was all about or why it should concern him.

Then the Dowager Countess said as if with an effort:

"To my husband all Artists were creatures apart, inferior socially and certainly not acceptable as a member of the O'Derry family."

At the word "artist" the Marquis sat bolt upright, his eyes on the Dowager Countess's face as he felt his heart pounding in his breast.

"What are you saying to me, Ma'am?" he asked.

Even to himself his voice sounded strange.

"I am explaining to you," the Dowager Countess replied, "what my husband and I felt when our only daughter ran away with a Miniaturist named Cornelius Lens, whose father had been expelled from Ireland as a devil-worshipper!"

"Vanessa is here with you?" the Marquis asked quickly.

It was the only thing that mattered: that Vanessa was safe, that he had found her!

"Yes, she is here," the Dowager Countess replied. "And she has told me that you wish to marry her. Is that true?"

"It is indeed!" the Marquis answered. "But I had no idea—none, Ma'am—that she was in any way connected with your family."

"Vanessa told me that," the Dowager Countess answered, "and she also told me that, until she learnt who her mother was, she did not consider it right or proper, considering your rank and position, for you to marry the daughter of an Artist."

"I once thought that of consequence, Ma'am," the Marquis said frankly, "but now it would not matter to me if Vanessa were the daughter of a crossing-sweeper! I love her and I intend to make her my wife!"

"With or without my approval, I suppose?" the Dowager Countess asked with a faint smile on her thin lips.

"Exactly, Ma'am!" the Marquis replied.

The Dowager Countess looked at him for a moment and he thought there was a twinkle in her eye.

"I can only hope, My Lord, that in the future you will be more careful about the company you keep. Vanessa would not, I am sure, feel at home with the type of person she would encounter at Carlton House."

"I will bear in mind what you have said, Ma'am," the Marquis said evasively. "May I see Vanessa?"

There was a youthful eagerness in the question which did not escape the Dowager Countess.

She seemed about to say something else, then she changed her mind, and picking up a small silver bell which stood on a table beside her she rang it.

Almost instantly the door opened and, thinking it to be a servant, the Marquis did not turn his head. Then when the Dowager Countess gave no command he looked round.

It was Vanessa who stood there just inside the door of the Drawing-Room, looking at him shyly and with an expression in her eyes which he thought was slightly apprehensive.

"Vanessa!"

The Marquis ejaculated her name in his deep voice as he rose to his feet.

The Dowager Countess also rose.

"It may be unconventional, My Lord," she said, "but I feel that you and my granddaughter have some things to explain to each other which are best said in private. I will leave you alone for ten minutes, but let me make one thing quite clear—there will be no secret marriage, no ceremony taking place with a Special Licence!"

Her voice softened as she went on:

"If you are both intent upon wedding each other, it will be from this house, where I intend to present my granddaughter to my friends after she has made her curtsey at Buckingham Palace!"

Having spoken, the Dowager Countess moved slowly and with great dignity across the Drawing-Room.

As she passed Vanessa she just touched her shoulder and it was, the Marquis knew, a gesture of affection.

The door closed behind her. Vanessa and the Marquis stood facing each other.

"Why could you not have told me?" the Marquis asked. "How could you have let me suffer such agony, thinking I had lost you again!"

"I would have left you a note," Vanessa answered, and there was no doubt about the apprehension in her eyes, "but I was not . . . certain if my Grandmother would . . . accept me. You see, I did not know she existed until Dorcas gave me the letter which my mother had written to me."

"What letter?" the Marquis asked.

His eyes were on Vanessa's face and he longed to take her in his arms; but he knew there were explanations to be made, although they were of no real consequence.

The only thing that mattered was that he had found her!

"Mama wanted more than anything else for me to be married for myself," Vanessa explained. "She never told me that she was an O'Derry. She had kept her identity a secret after running away with Papa because she feared her father might pursue her."

She gave a little wistful smile as she said:

"Actually, Grandmama tells me that my Grandfather wiped her out of his life after she disappeared. He was an autocrat and would not stand for disobedience amongst his children."

"So you did not know who your mother's family were?" the Marquis asked.

"She never spoke of them except to say that she

had been forced to run away with Papa," Vanessa explained, "and because it upset him we never talked about it. Then before she . . . died she wrote me a long letter, and she made Dorcas promise not to give it to me until I wished to marry and had already . . . accepted the man who had . . . offered for me."

She blushed a little at the words and the Marquis said softly:

"So you did mean to marry me?"

"I knew that if you . . . went on . . . asking me I would find . . . it impossible to say . . . no," Vanessa replied.

They looked into each other's eyes and the world stood still. Then with an effort the Marquis said:

"Will you tell me what your mother wrote?"

"She explained that she was aware that the man chosen for her by her father was not in the least in love with her. There was another woman in his life, but he wanted to be linked with the O'Derry family. He was not at all interested in Mama for herself."

"So she ran away with your father?"

"She had fallen very much in love with him and, although he was older, he was desperately in love with her, as I have told you before, and they were very, very happy."

"As we shall be!"

Vanessa looked up at the Marquis and her eyes were full of sunshine.

"You sound very . . . sure of . . . that."

"I am!"

He made a little movement as if he would pull her to him. But feeling that they must first finish what they were saying to each other, he asked:

"Your mother told you in her letter that your Grandmother was the Dowager Countess of Clanderry. But how did you know where to find her?"

"When I read the name in my mother's letter," Vanessa answered, "it seemed to ring a bell in my mind. Then suddenly I remembered that, when the Duchess of Tealby spoke to me when I was staying with you at Ruckford Park, she said that if I would go back to London she would get me some small commissions."

"I have told the Duchess what I think of her and her commissions!" the Marquis interposed.

"I recalled her saying that the Dowager Countess of Clanderry, who lived in Berkeley Square, wanted a portrait of her favourite dog."

"So that is how you knew where to find your Grandmother?"

"It was not difficult when we reached Berkeley Square to find her house. It is nearly as big as yours!"

"So now you have a Grandmother and, I imagine, innumerable Irish relations?" the Marquis said.

He paused and then added with laughter in his voice:

"As your Grandmother pointed out to me very firmly, the O'Derrys are a far older and far more important family than the Ruckfords. Are you quite certain you would not do better to wait for a more distinguished applicant for your hand?"

Vanessa moved towards him and his arms went round her.

"Please . . . will you marry me?" she pleaded. "And will you . . . forgive me for . . . worrying you?"

"I will forgive you for your first disappearance," the Marquis replied, holding her closely against him, "but since you found your Grandmother yesterday morning, why did you not send a message to me last night or at least first thing today? I have never spent such a miserable twenty-four hours!"

To his surprise, Vanessa blushed and turned her face against his shoulder.

The Marquis put his hand under her chin and turned her face up to his.

"Tell me the truth," he demanded. "Why the delay? Were you deliberately punishing me for my sins, of which I am very ashamed?"

"No, no, of course not!" Vanessa cried, "it was just . . ."

She paused and as her eyes flickered he saw the darkness of her lashes against her cheeks.

"What was the reason?" he insisted.

"You said that our 'frames' were not . . . important,'" Vanessa murmured, "but yours is so . . . magnificent and I did want to have a . . . new gown before you saw me."

For a moment the Marquis was astonished. Then he laughed.

"A new gown! My precious darling, as if it mattered! Do you not realise that to me you have always been framed in dreams?"

He held her closer still and now very gently his lips found hers.

He kissed her as he had done the night on the terrace and once again the magical feeling of belonging swept over them both.

His kisses grew more insistent, more demanding, more possessive, and as he felt her quiver in his arms he knew that they were indivisible—a part of each other, and nothing and nobody could ever separate them.

It did not matter who Vanessa was or what blood flowed in his veins. They were a man and a woman who had been meant for each other since the beginning of time and would seek each other through all eternity.

They were not two people but one, and, whatever difficulties or problems lay ahead, the only thing that mattered was that they were together.

The Marquis raised his head.

"I love you, my darling! I love you until it is impossible to think of anything except you and my love for you."

"That is what I have always felt for you," Vanessa whispered. "When you kiss me, I feel that my lips are yours and so is my whole body. But it is impossible to think, only to feel that our love is perfect."

"It is perfect!" the Marquis answered. "Just as ever since we met you have brought me the perfection I have been seeking all my life in your delicacy, your grace, your sweetness, and above all the wonder of your eyes."

He held her very close as he said:

"It was the portrait of an eye that enabled me to find you at Vauxhall, for which I shall always be grateful. All I want now is to look into your eyes, my darling, because they mirror the beauty of your heart and soul and they tell me of things I have never known before."

"I think there are . . . things hidden . . . deep in both of us," Vanessa answered, "that are put there by God, and which will become part of our happiness."

"There is so much for us to search for, to learn, and to enjoy," the Marquis said in his deep voice.

Then as if he could not help himself he kissed Vanessa again, kissing her now frantically, as if the fears he had suffered these past weeks could only be assuaged by her softness, her pliability, her closeness.

"I love you!" he said at length, and Vanessa knew that it was a vow more than an expression of his feelings.

He drew a deep breath and then he said, his voice a little unsteady:

"How soon can we be married? I want you, my darling. I want you close to me. It will be agony to leave you, even though I know you will be safe with your Grandmother and just across the Square."

"We shall have to persuade Grandmama that we are in a hurry!" Vanessa said.

"I have never known such a feeling of urgency as I have now," the Marquis answered, and he was not smiling.

"She is so pleased to have me here," Vanessa said, "but I am sure she will do anything we ask! I think really she admires you even though she disapproves of the life you have led up to now."

"I promise that I will turn over a new leaf!"

"I do not want you to change. I want you just as you are," Vanessa told him, a note of adoration in her voice.

"Is that the truth?"

"Look into my eyes and you will see for yourself."

The Marquis looked down at her and kissed her eyes, one after another, then the tip of her small straight nose, her cheeks, and once again her lips.

"When we are married," he said, "I will kiss you all over your adorable body so that every inch of you becomes mine."

He felt her tremble at the passion in his voice and went on:

"But I cannot wait for long, my darling little love. I want you as I have never wanted anything or anyone in my whole life, and every day that we are not together, every hour that you are not close to me, every minute that I am not kissing you, is wasted and lost."

"Let us go and talk to Grandmama now," Vanessa suggested, and he knew that she was moved by his urgency.

He kissed her again, then taking his arms from round her he put his hands on her shoulders and said:

"Now let me look at this gown of dreams for which I paid a very high price in suffering and misery!"

"It was . . . wrong of me," Vanessa said, "please . . . please forgive me!"

He looked into her eyes and it was impossible to look down at what she was wearing.

Instead, once again he pulled her roughly against him and his mouth took possession of hers.

He felt the fire burning fiercely within him arouse a response, and a flame rose within her. He felt the softness of her lips quivering beneath the insistence of his.

Then he lifted her up into a starlit sky and there were only themselves and their dream of love, which would encompass, sustain, and inspire them all their lives.

ABOUT THE AUTHOR

BARBARA CARTLAND, the celebrated romantic author, historian, playwright, lecturer, political speaker and television personality, has now written over 150 books. Miss Cartland has had a number of historical books published and several biographical ones, including that of her brother, Major Ronald Cartland, who was the first Member of Parliament to be killed in the War. This book had a Foreword by Sir Winston Churchill.

In private life, Barbara Cartland, who is a Dame of the Order of St. John of Jerusalem, has fought for better conditions and salaries for Midwives and nurses. As President of the Royal College of Midwives (Hertfordshire Branch), she has been invested with the first Badge of Office ever given in Great Britain, which was subscribed to by the Midwives themselves. She has also championed the cause for old people and founded the first Romany Gypsy Camp in the world.

Barbara Cartland is deeply interested in Vitamin Therapy and is President of the British National Association for Health.

Barbara Cartland

The world's bestselling author of romantic fiction.
Her stories are always captivating tales of intrigue,
adventure and love.

☐	THE TEARS OF LOVE	2148	$1.25
☐	THE BORED BRIDEGROOM	6381	$1.25
☐	JOURNEY TO PARADISE	6383	$1.25
☐	THE PENNILESS PEER	6387	$1.25
☐	NO DARKNESS FOR LOVE	6427	$1.25
☐	THE LITTLE ADVENTURE	6428	$1.25
☐	THE SHADOW OF SIN	6430	$1.25
☐	LESSONS IN LOVE	6431	$1.25
☐	THE DARING DECEPTION	6435	$1.25
☐	CASTLE OF FEAR	8103	$1.25
☐	THE GLITTERING LIGHTS	8104	$1.25
☐	A SWORD TO THE HEART	8105	$1.25
☐	THE KARMA OF LOVE	8106	$1.25
☐	THE MAGNIFICENT MARRIAGE	8166	$1.25
☐	THE RUTHLESS RAKE	8240	$1.25
☐	THE DANGEROUS DANDY	8280	$1.25
☐	THE WICKED MARQUIS	8467	$1.25
☐	THE FRIGHTENED BRIDE	8780	$1.25
☐	THE FLAME IS LOVE	8887	$1.25